BELLA'S HEART

LEGACY SERIES
BOOK 9

PAULA KAY

CONTENTS

ONE

Isabella gave a start in her chair at the feel of Thomas's hand on her back.

"Hey. How was your walk?" she asked. "You were out early this morning."

Thomas leaned down to give her a quick kiss on the lips before he sat in the chair next to her. "Great. Would you believe that I jogged a little?"

"Did you?" Isabella got up from her own chair to sit on Thomas's lap, wrapping her arms around his neck and teasing him with her smile. "Does that mean you're ready to go for a run with me? I was just about to take a break."

"Were you now?" Thomas leaned in to give her a deep kiss, momentarily causing her to forget any ideas about running or finishing the current chapter she was writing.

Isabella moved back into her own chair and reached for Thomas's hand across the small table as she looked out toward the sea. "I'm still in awe of our view here." She felt the familiar ache that she'd been having lately at the thought of their travels ending. "Thomas, are we really going to leave our little island paradise next week?"

Thomas looked at her intently before replying to the question that Isabella already knew the answer to.

Traveling with Thomas the past seven months had been a dream. From the moment he'd surprised her at the villa over Christmas—from the moment he'd finally kissed her again—the two had been inseparable. It had been just like old times with her best friend, only everything was different.

Thomas loved her, and it was in a way that made everything magical and intense for Isabella.

Spending time in Paris again had been incredible and romantic. Isabella had put her writing on hold to do all the tourist things she hadn't done the first time around. And then they'd gone on to Spain and Portugal, the weeks turning into months, their travels taking them to Eastern Europe and then Turkey.

They'd decided to end their time traveling together with a month long stay in Greece, and Isabella was loving everything about her time in Santorini. She'd finally gotten back into a morning writing groove and her afternoons with Thomas had been spent lounging at the beach, eating delicious Mediterranean salads and talking about everything they'd seen and done.

Isabella turned her attention back to Thomas, who was nudging her gently in the side.

"Huh? Sorry, what was that?"

He laughed as he brought her hair back and kissed her neck just below her ear in a way that always made her forget her thoughts momentarily.

He reached for her hand and turned her just slightly in his lap so that it was easier for Isabella to look him in the eye.

"I was just saying that you don't have to leave, Iz. It's me that needs to return to New York next week—to the grind of hitting the books again—but I hate for you to give up your tra—"

"Stop." Isabella's voice interrupted Thomas right before she planted a kiss squarely on his mouth. "I am going back with you. We've already decided." She studied him intently for a few seconds.

It was shocking how attracted she was to this man who had been such a big part of her life for so many years. She still had to pinch herself at times that the two of them had actually taken such a huge leap in their relationship. He was the same goofy Thomas who'd always made her laugh, who'd always practically known her thoughts before she'd even uttered a word. Yet, so much had changed.

In the months that they'd been together as more than just friends, sometimes Isabella had to force the doubts away. Way in the back of her mind was the tiniest idea that she could wake up one day to realize that it wasn't the same for Thomas as it was for her. That she wasn't, in fact, the love of his life—not in the same way that she was sure he was for her.

But she had no reason to think that. Thomas had done nothing but reassure her of the intensity of his feelings, and she loved him all the more for knowing that she needed that from him.

"But?" Thomas kissed the tip of her nose.

"But what?"

"I know there's a but there, Iz, so just tell me what it is." He laughed, but Isabella's heart was racing slightly and she felt very serious all of a sudden.

She looked him in the eye. "Thomas, do you want me to come to New York? I mean, you'd tell me if you didn't, right?" She held her breath in as she waited for him to answer her.

It wasn't that they hadn't had lengthy discussions about it—they had. Somewhere between graduating high school and during the months of his travels with Isabella, Thomas had suddenly become more serious than he'd ever been about school. It was a side of him that Isabella hadn't really seen before—not while they'd been in high school together, anyway. It was she who was the more studious one, while Thomas hadn't really put any pressure on himself when it came to homework and his grades.

But Thomas was naturally smart, and getting into NYU had seemed to mature him in ways that were attractive to Isabella. It was quite the role reversal actually—somewhat amusing when she really stopped to think about it. When she'd brought up the subject of Thomas postponing school to travel longer, she'd found out just how serious he was, and she couldn't fault him for it.

Thomas pulled her toward him and Isabella nestled her face close under his chin, as he squeezed her tighter. "Iz, of course I want you there with me. That's not a question at all. The idea of not being able to see you every day disturbs me greatly." He laughed.

"Really?" She turned in his lap again so she could see his face.

"Really. But..."

"Oh, I see. Now, who's the one with a but, mister?" Her voice was light, but inside she felt concern. Was there a but about her going back to New York with him?

"Come on, Iz. I just want to be sure it's what you want. I'd hate to think that you'd be giving up your dreams of travel for me. I mean, that's a lot of pressure for a guy." He laughed. "I'm not at all sure what it's going to be like, but you've already said that you want to get your own place—that you don't want us to live together—so I'm not really sure how much actual time we'll be able to spend together."

They had discussed living together. It was Thomas who'd suggested it. After all, they were living together now during their travels, he'd said. But, for whatever reason, Isabella was old-fashioned when it came to that part of their relationship—the physical part. They'd been affectionate with one another and she loved how affectionate he was with her, but Isabella wasn't ready for that next step yet.

When she'd told Thomas that a big part of her wanted to wait —maybe even until she was married one day—he'd kissed her so sweetly and told her that he loved her—that he loved everything about her. She knew that Thomas wouldn't pressure her whether they lived together or not, but she couldn't see the point of making it more difficult on either of them; and living together in a real long-term New York apartment felt a little too much like playing house to her.

So they'd decided that Isabella would stay with him—just at first—while she figured out her own living situation. She hadn't exactly expressed her own doubts to Thomas—everything had changed so quickly that her head was still swimming with all that had happened. She didn't doubt their relationship, but when it came to her actually living in New York, she'd be lying to herself if she said that she was completely comfortable with the idea. She could write from anywhere, and the large inheritance that she'd received from her birth mother—from Arianna—allowed her the freedom to give it a try anyway. So there didn't seem to be a reason not to—not when she couldn't bear the thought of being on her own, without Thomas, after so many wonderful memories they had from their travels together.

She turned her attention back to Thomas, who seemed to be waiting for some kind of reply from her. She'd been so scattered lately. Had there been a question?

"Sorry, what did you say?"

Thomas laughed. "Babe, you really are a million miles away this morning." He moved her gently off his lap. "I was just saying that we don't really know what my schedule is going to be like with school and everything. I just don't want you to be disappointed if I don't have much time to spend with you during the week, ya know?"

Isabella nodded. "I know. I do get that. We won't know until we try it, I guess. Right?"

"That's right." Thomas leaned over to give her a quick kiss on the lips. "And now, my darling, I am going to go grab a quick shower. Are you gonna go for that run?"

Isabella grinned. "Yep. I think a run will clear this cloudy distracted brain of mine. Then do you want to hit the beach with me afterward—lunch and a swim?"

"It's a date."

TWO

Isabella took long even breaths in as she listened to the sound of her feet hitting the dirt trail. She'd been delighted to discover a path from their villa that led down and along the sea for a good three miles in one direction. She was finally getting to the point where she could almost complete the six miles there and back without slowing to a walk—something that would have been a piece of cake for her a year ago.

Both she and Thomas had been loving their time in Santorini. It really was as magical and picturesque as what she'd imagined when they'd booked their stay in the villa. The buildings were a crisp white against the backdrop of so many beautiful shades of blue—the dark blue domes that topped the structures, the turquoise blue of the clear sea, and the unclouded light blue of the sky. Yes, their Greek island stay had been everything she'd hoped for and more.

Isabella felt her heart lurch as it always did lately when she thought of leaving. She loved the way things had been between her and Thomas throughout their travels together. Going back to New York signified going back to real life—or at least a new reality for them both—and she didn't want their little romance bubble to burst.

She wished that she could express her fears to Thomas but something stopped her. She didn't want to be needy or untrusting, but inside she still couldn't completely accept the fact that what had happened between them wasn't going to go away. And deep down she felt herself holding back a bit for the fear of it.

She shook her head as if doing so would push any negative thoughts away as she began to make her way up the one challenging part of the trail. As she reached the top of incline, she saw the bright pink of a woman's baseball cap in the distance just before the woman stumbled and fell to the ground, her speed seeming to catapult her off the trail a good distance as she fell forward.

Isabella took off at full speed as soon as she realized what she'd seen, crossing the distance between them in seconds.

"Are you okay?" She peered down at the woman now in a sitting position with her hands around her ankle.

"Oh, hey. I'll bet that looked graceful." She laughed and then seemed to wince slightly as she looked up at Isabella.

Isabella carefully took the few steps needed to bend down next to her, eyeing the ankle that was already very swollen and a light shade of purple. "Do you think it's broken?" She reached into the small bag she wore to pull out the little first aid kit she carried with her—pretty much at all times. Thomas had teased her about it, right before he'd kissed her and said that it was kinda nice to see some of the "always prepared Izzy" that he'd known from back home.

"How annoying. That will teach me not to run and play with my music at that same time."

Isabella reached down to offer the woman her hand. "Do you want to try to stand? See if you can put any weight on it at all?" She smiled as the woman reached up to take her hand. "I'm Is— I'm Bella, by the way."

Isabella leaned down to put her other hand around the woman's shoulder, giving her more support as she stood up.

"Thanks. And I'm Nina." She winced again as she allowed Isabella to help her into a standing position.

"Good to meet you, Nina. I wish it were under better circumstances." She squeezed Nina's hand. "Okay, now lean into me if you need to and let's just see if you can put any weight at all on your foot. Take your time."

Nina gingerly put her foot down in front of her, then let it take most of her weight as she stepped forward with the other. "Okay, it's painful, but it doesn't seem to be broken, thank God."

Isabella nodded her head, noticing the blood dripping down Nina's leg. "Okay. That's great. Do you think you can make it to that big rock over there? I have something to clean your scrape and I just happen to have a bandage that we can use to wrap your ankle."

Nina laughed. "You're really prepared, aren't you?"

"I guess I am." Isabella laughed too. "Well, I've been traveling a bit and I wasn't too sure about the things that I'd be needing while away from home."

The two made their way over to the big boulder and Nina sat down with her leg stretched out in front of her. Isabella knelt down, pouring some water from her water bottle unto the scrape just below Nina's knee. She reached into her bag, pulling out a small container of alcohol and the biggest band-aid she had, and carefully cleaned the scrape before applying the band-aid.

Nina seemed to be studying her carefully. "I feel pretty lucky that you happened to be behind me on the trail today. I just arrived here yesterday but someone from my hotel told me that it can be pretty quiet out on this trail."

"It's true. I run here nearly every day—well, for the past three weeks or so. Hmm, there's a little cafe just around the next corner down toward the beach. Do you think you can make it that far? Is there someone we can call to pick you up?"

"Yes, I think I'll be fine to walk and no, there's no one to come pick me up. I'm flying solo these days—footloose and fancy free, I guess you could say." She laughed lightly.

"Great. Well, let me wrap this bandage around your ankle. That should help give you some support, and then we really do need to get some ice on it right away."

"You look pretty young to be a doctor." Nina winked.

Isabella laughed. "Four years of track—with my own share of injuries." She tucked the clasp into the fabric of the bandage. "There, how does that feel?"

Nina stood up and carefully hobbled a few steps. "Okay. So, I'm not gonna win any races, but maybe I'll be okay to actually enjoy some time at the beach—one can hope, anyway."

Isabella moved back to where Nina had been on the ground to collect her MP3 player and her one sneaker, before the two made their way slowly along the path. "Well, I hope this won't ruin your vacation. How long are you here for?"

"Oh, well, it's not really a vacation. I mean, it is, but sort of a working one, I guess you'd say."

"Oh? Can I ask what you do? That sounds interesting, and I suppose it's been something I've been trying out for myself."

"I'm a photographer—and a bit of a travel blogger, but mostly it's about the images for me. And it's fairly new for me too."

Isabella tried to study Nina discreetly. She felt drawn to her—fascinated about this woman, who in just a few words, seemed to stir up all kinds of emotions and questions within her. If she had to guess, she'd say that Nina seemed to be in her early thirties. She was tanned and looked to be in very good shape. There was something about her—about the way that she had laughed despite the obvious pain and frustration she'd been in earlier—that made Isabella want to know more about her.

"I'd love to hear more about what you do—if you don't mind. It sounds very interesting to me."

"Sure. Let me buy you a coffee and we'll swap stories while we get some ice on this bad boy. You seem so young. I'd love to hear what you're doing at this little piece of paradise—and for weeks at that? I get the feeling that you're not on the average gap year backpacking trip with your buddies."

Isabella smiled as the last months flashed through her mind—getting that first phone call from Douglas, meeting her grandparents and her wonderful new extended family in Italy, and all of the many hours she'd sat reading and rereading her birth mother's journals.

No, she certainly hadn't been on just any ordinary budget backpacking trip. Isabella's whole world as she knew it had shifted, thanks to a mother she'd never had the chance to know—thanks to Arianna and her dreams for a daughter she'd only held for a moment as an infant.

Her thoughts turned toward Thomas and their upcoming move to New York as she sent him a quick text.

And her whole world was about to shift again, and for some reason, Isabella didn't know how she was feeling about that.

THREE

Isabella helped Nina to get her foot settled on the chair with the bag of ice that the cafe owner had rushed to get for them. As the waitress delivered their coffees to the table, Isabella felt Nina's gaze on her.

"Bella, thanks so much—for everything. I guess I was pretty lucky that you happened to be out on the path near me this morning. I'm not quite sure how I would have managed without you."

"Oh, you're welcome. I'm glad I was able to help. How's it feeling now, by the way? Any better?"

Nina leaned forward and lifted the bag of ice slightly. "I think it's not actually going to be as bad as I first thought. The swelling seems to already be going down a bit." She took a sip of her coffee and sat back again in her chair. "So tell me about you. Are you here alone or with friends?"

"Yeah, I'm here with my best—with my boyfriend." Isabella could feel the instant warmth in her cheeks and knew that she must be beet red.

Nina laughed. "Well, is your boyfriend also your best friend? Because that sounds pretty good to me."

"Yeah, he was—he is, actually. Sorry, I don't know why it's so weird to talk about. It's a new thing and—well—somewhat unexpected, I guess."

"Well, that sure does sound pretty exciting. I'm game if you wanna share? Or I don't want to keep you either. He's probably waiting for you."

"Oh no, I was thinking, actually—maybe I'll text him to come meet us here? In a while, I mean. We have a rental car, so we can take you back to your hotel."

"You're too kind. And thank you for that. I think I'll be spending the rest of the day with my foot up, so I'll take you up on your offer."

Isabella texted Thomas, and then she easily talked to Nina for the next thirty minutes—almost non-stop. She filled her in about her travels, Thomas, the highlights of her family, and how she had come to be in Europe to begin with. She sat back in her chair, suddenly feeling bad for monopolizing so much of the conversation. It wasn't like her and she wasn't quite sure why she would open up to a perfect stranger like she had. But something about Nina made her feel completely comfortable. She took a quick sip of her coffee.

"Wow, I'm so sorry to go on and on like that. What I really want is to hear all about you. The fact that you're traveling as a photographer is very fascinating to me."

Nina reached out to lightly touch Isabella's arm. "Oh, don't be silly. There's nothing to be sorry about. Your life sounds absolutely incredible—everything that has happened to you in such a short amount of time. Your head must still be spinning a bit from it all. And Thomas—now I can't wait to meet this lifelong friend of yours, who sounds absolutely dreamy."

"So, what about you? I mean, I know you're here alone but is there someone back home? Where is home for you, by the way?"

Isabella saw just the quickest flash of something pass across Nina's face, but when she looked back at her, the smile was still there.

"So, let's see...I'm originally from the Midwest—near Chicago. But I moved to California when I was just out of my first year of college—chasing the dream of stardom, I suppose." She laughed. "Most recently, I'd been living in San Francisco, and to answer your other question, no—there's no one at home waiting for me to come back. I married my husband—sorry—my ex-husband—nearly ten years ago and our divorce was finalized six months ago." She lifted her phone up, looking at it for a few seconds. "Actually, it will be exactly six months in two days from now."

"Oh, I'm sorry. And I don't mean to pry." Isabella felt bad for having brought the subject up.

"Oh, please. Don't be sorry. It was the best thing to have happened to me in the last eleven years." Nina laughed. "Things between us weren't good. I should have known better, I suppose."

"So you were pretty young, I guess, when you got married."

"I guess—but I don't think thirty is so young—old enough to know better, anyway, right?" She winked at Isabella across the table.

"Wait. Really? That means you're—" Isabella stopped herself, feeling her face grow warm again.

Nina laughed again and Isabella recognized that, though she'd only known this woman for less than a few hours, it was what drew her to want to know so much more about Nina. Her laugh and demeanor was light and full of life. It was hard for Isabella to conceive of the fact that this woman sitting across from her had only recently gone through a break-up as major as a divorce.

"It's true. I just turned forty pretty recently—thus, my whole leaving to travel the world and find myself routine."

Isabella looked at Nina intently. Her words might indicate a crisis of sorts, but Isabella didn't think Nina meant them seriously. She certainly didn't look like a woman in crisis—well, apart from her swollen ankle up on a chair.

"Well, I never would have thought you to be forty—I mean, you look really fantastic. And not that being forty is bad or anything." Isabella willed herself to stop talking. She seemed to keep sticking her foot in her mouth, but across from her, Nina only grinned.

"Oh, don't be silly. You're too kind. And compared to you, I know I must seem ancient, but I'm determined to make my forties absolutely the best decade of my life. Well, I'll have fun trying, anyway—if I can keep myself from fatal injury, that is."

"That sounds like a great goal—on both counts. And what about your travels? I'd love to hear where you've been and where you're headed to next. And how you're making everything fit together with your work also. That's so fascinating to me."

Nina's whole face lit up as she settled back into her chair. "Have you been to Thailand yet, Bella?"

Isabella shook her head as she thought about Arianna's map pinned up on the wall back at the villa where she and Thomas were staying. She—along with Jemma and then Thomas—had made great strides in her goal to try to recreate at least part of the dream that her birth mother had had to see the world. Somewhere along the way during the past months of travel, Arianna's dream had become Isabella's dream.

She loved how travel seemed to stretch her. She knew that the way she traveled was privileged compared to a lot of other young people backpacking and staying in youth hostels around the globe, but that didn't mean that her way of travel wasn't causing her to grow. She'd mostly been in Europe though, and the allure of Southeast Asia did intrigue her whenever she looked at it on the map. What had the draw been for her mother? And Nina?

She turned her attention back to the woman sitting across from her. "No, I've not been to Thailand, but it is on my list. I'd love to hear all about it."

Just then, Isabella saw Thomas enter the cafe. She grinned up at him as he approached where they were sitting at the table but inside she felt slightly disappointed that her time alone with Nina was ending.

"Hi, I hope that I'm not interrupting you two. I'm Thomas." He stuck his hand out toward Nina.

"Thomas, this is Nina." Isabella smiled as the two shook hands and Nina removed the ice from her ankle so that she could take her foot off the chair next to her.

"Great to meet you, Thomas. I've heard a lot of lovely things about you," said Nina.

"How's your ankle doing? Don't stop what you're doing with it on account of my arrival," said Thomas.

Isabella bent down to look closer at Nina's ankle. "It's looking better, isn't it? How does it feel now?"

Nina stood up, shifting her weight to her injured foot. "It feels tons better. I think I will actually be able to walk on it just fine." She glanced at Isabella. "Well, maybe after a full day of resting it."

"I think that's a good idea—to rest it, at least for the remainder of the day," said Isabella.

"Yes, and on that note, I don't want to keep you two from enjoying this romantic island together any longer than I already have, so we can go whenever you're ready. And thank you so much, Thomas, for coming to give me a lift. That's very kind of you."

"It's no problem at all."

"So Nina, I would love to hear more about your travels and Thailand, though—when you're feeling up to it—and if that would work for you."

"Yes, I'd love to get together again before we both leave. Absolutely, because we still have tons left to talk about it." Nina grinned.

Isabella and Nina exchanged e-mail addresses, with the promise to be in touch over the next few days.

FOUR

Isabella felt Thomas watching her intently as she scooped a bite of salad into her mouth. She kicked him lightly under the table with her bare foot. "What are you looking at?"

Thomas leaned in to kiss her on the cheek. "You look so intense. Like you have a million thoughts racing through that brilliant beautiful mind of yours."

Isabella laughed. "I'm sorry. I suppose I'm thinking about Nina and this morning. She seems so interesting. I really do hope that I can spend a little more time with her before she leaves. She mentioned Thailand to me and it's really got me thinking about Southeast Asia again. When we might go, I mean."

Thomas was quiet. "Iz, I might be able to get away during spring break, but I'm not sure that Asia is going to be very logical for only a week's trip."

"Oh, I know. Never mind. I just want to hear more about her and the work she's doing. I know that we'll need to wait until summer for any real travel plans again. You know that I fully support you when it comes to your studies." Isabella leaned over to touch Thomas's arm from across the table. "You do know that, don't you?"

"Yes, I do. And you know that I also support any travel aspirations that you have."

Isabella looked down toward her plate of food, suddenly desperate to change the subject. She and Thomas had already talked about her travels, his school, and living in New York until there didn't seem anything left to say about the topic. Now whenever it came up, it only seemed to make Isabella feel uncomfortable. She couldn't quite put her finger on the reasons why, and she only wanted to avoid the topic except for where she left it alone in her own head.

"Iz?"

"Yeah?"

"I don't mean to keep bringing it up, but I think it's important that we're clear with one another. Don't you?"

"Yes, of course. But what do you mean? Clear about what exactly?"

"Well, I just don't want you to have any regrets—the last thing I'd want is for you to feel like you are giving something up for me. I know we've talked about it but then when I see you mention travel ideas that you have—it just makes me feel like maybe coming to New York is not going to be what's best for you. And I wouldn't fault you for that."

"Oh, I know, Thomas. And I'm sorry. You don't need to worry about that. I promise I'm going to try my best to make the best decisions for both of us. All we can do is try it, right? Do I still have travel that I want to do? Yes. But if I'm being honest, I don't want to do it without you. So I'll just have to wait until summer or whenever you can—"

"But Iz, you shouldn't have to wait. That's my point. It's not fair to you."

"Thomas, I want to be with you. Let's just drop it for now, okay? The water looks so wonderful. I'm dying to get in there. Are you almost finished?"

They were eating Greek salads at one of their favorite cafes just steps from the beach. They would often dine at one of the tables with an umbrella above them and the sand under their feet. An order of drinks or food would hold the spot for them all afternoon as they came and went from the sea at their leisure.

"Yeah, and okay, we can drop it for now. Just promise me one thing, Iz."

"What's that?"

Thomas took her hand in both of his. "Once we get there—to New York—you have to promise me that you'll be honest with me and with yourself about how you're feeling, okay? I don't want to have to wonder if it's really the best decision for you. Your happiness means something to me too, you know."

Isabella got up from the table to come around and pull Thomas up to his feet. Reaching her hands up around his neck, she pulled him in for a big hug. "That's a promise."

Thomas smiled at her as he kissed her quickly on the top of her head. "Great, now last one in has to buy lunch."

Isabella laughed as she took off running across the beach after him.

Isabella loved the sensation of weightlessness that she felt bobbing around in the sea. It still surprised her that she could float around out there for hours without tiring of it. She loved watching the mostly European families that dotted the beach—families and couples away for the entire last month of the summer—one last hurrah before it was back to work and the day-to-day living that was catching up with them all.

One thing that she'd really come to love about her stay in much of southern Europe was the attitude toward work and life. She'd felt it greatly in Spain and Italy—that love for food, wine, and friends. The way that entire communities seemed to shut down for long lunches and siestas and then revive for long hours and late dinners well into the nights. Life had felt slower-paced and very content as she watched the people where she and Thomas had traveled.

It couldn't be helped that Isabella was already comparing it to what she imagined life back in New York was going to be. America, and especially the big city, was about as fast-paced as any place she could imagine. Was she truly ready for that type of lifestyle? Even thinking about it reminded her of her last year in high school. Had it really only been a year since she'd been frantically wrapping up her exams, track, and everything else that had been going on in her busy life back then?

Thomas's arm around her brought Isabella out of her thoughts. She kissed him playfully on the lips and then dove down into the water, pulling him with her.

They both came to the surface sputtering and laughing as Thomas smoothed the hair back from her face. "So, you didn't really tell me about Nina—about her work and what it was about her that seems to have you so distracted today."

"Yeah, so we didn't really get a chance to talk about it much, but she's a photographer and I think she has her own travel blog. Interesting, right?"

"Mm-hm. She did seem very nice. Is she here alone then?"

"Yes, that we did discuss just a bit. She's only recently divorced —she seems to be on a little sabbatical of sorts, I guess you could call it. I'll definitely connect with her—about the work. Maybe she has some tips for me about working while traveling. You know I haven't had the easiest time of balancing it all during my travels."

"Yeah, but you've not really had a good reason to—or a need to, I should say."

Isabella felt herself tense up just a bit. "What do you mean?"

"Well, I just mean that you don't really need to do it for money —what with the big trust that Arianna left you."

The look on Thomas's face made Isabella think that he felt bad about what he'd blurted out.

"But, I don't mean to say that your writing isn't important, Iz. I know that it is."

"No. I know what you mean." Isabella smiled in the hopes of Thomas not seeing what she was feeling all of a sudden. "Getting everything from Arianna did change my life. There's no denying that. It certainly has made things a lot easier for me in terms of finances, that's for sure. But I still want to do something and right now that something would appear to be writing."

Thomas leaned over to kiss her again. "And you're a great writer, Iz. Of course you should be doing that—figuring out how to make it work for you. And you will. I'm sure of it."

Isabella smiled in response. "And on that note, I suppose I should get back, because I do want to finish writing the section that I started this morning. How 'bout you? Ready to get out? I don't mind walking back if you want to stay longer."

"I think I'll swim a little. You go ahead and take the car. I'll walk back."

"Okay, see you in a bit."

FIVE

Isabella and Nina walked in easy silence for a few minutes. It was a perfect day to be out for a short hike on the trail that followed along the beach, and Isabella was still shocked at how quickly Nina had gotten back on her feet. The two women had already exchanged numerous e-mails and shared a few meals with one another since they'd met nearly a week before. And Isabella felt that a true friendship had been forged between them.

"So how are you feeling about leaving tomorrow? I really hope that Thomas doesn't mind me stealing you away this morning..."

"Oh, no. I think he has some romantic dinner planned for us. Probably at my favorite place in town. And we'll have one last swim this afternoon together also."

"Uh-oh. That look."

"That noticeable, huh?" Isabella had been having a hard time as the days grew closer and closer to their leaving. She kept telling Thomas that she would be fine, but inside, her emotions were a mess.

"Hey, I get it. I won't be happy to leave this paradise myself."

"And remind me where you are off to next?" Isabella had had long chats with Nina about her travels, and was completely enamored by her new friend's lifestyle and the beautiful photographs that Nina had shared with her since they'd met.

"I think I'll go back to Italy. Your description of Tuscany has me realizing that I missed something really beautiful when I was there. But I am thinking about extending my stay here by a few weeks first. I haven't quite gotten around the island the way that I'd intended, and I don't want to leave without getting some shots of the other side."

"Well, do be careful on that Vespa you rented." Isabella laughed. "I don't want to hear about any more tumbles after I've gone."

"You don't have to worry about that. From now on, safety first is my motto." Nina glanced over at Isabella, looking like she wanted to say something else.

"What? Why do I get the feeling you have something to say to me?" Isabella laughed lightly. She'd really surprised herself with how quickly she'd opened up to her new friend, and she quite enjoyed the easy way that they seemed to have with one another.

"Have you thought any more about what we talked about the other day? About Thailand?"

During lunch the day before, Nina had shared her Southeast Asia photos with Isabella and they'd talked for hours about Nina's time in Thailand—what she'd described to Isabella as three life-changing months of her life.

Isabella stopped to bend down to tie her shoe. She had been thinking about Thailand and about leaving Greece and about what her new life was going to be like in New York. It was all that she'd been thinking about lately. But she didn't know if she was able to verbalize the uneasiness she was feeling. She definitely hadn't wanted to approach it—again—with Thomas. It only served to validate his concerns about the decision that Isabella was making to stop her travels.

Isabella stretched her arms high above her head while Nina stood nearby watching her.

"Well, I do admit that I'm even more curious about Thailand now—that's for sure. But..."

"Yes? But what?"

"Oh, but nothing. Maybe we'll go this summer—during Thomas's summer break. I'll have to talk to him more about it—once we're settled—once he's settled at school and everything."

"You'd have much better weather if you went in the fall—well, in the north, anyway, it will be lovely. You'll run into lots of rain in the summer, depending on where you choose to go."

"Winter is definitely not going to work. Nothing will work, really, until summer, so I guess it's better to just table the idea for now." Isabella's voice sounded strained, even to her own ear, but suddenly she felt like dropping the subject of future travel with her friend.

Nina reached out to take Isabella's hand, leading her toward a bench off the side of the path. "Let's sit down and chat for a minute, shall we?"

Isabella sat and tried to control the tears that threatened out of nowhere. She didn't know why she felt upset exactly, but she knew that she didn't want Nina to witness her tears—not today anyway.

"Bella, what is it? What has you so upset?"

Isabella took a deep breath and let the tears fall. "Oh, I don't know. I'm trying to be okay with everything—be supportive of Thomas—but..."

"But what if you want something else? Something different than what Thomas wants right now?"

Isabella nodded her head. "But also, I don't want to go to Thailand—or anywhere, really—by myself. Nina, I don't think I'm as brave as you are. I mean, I only just got over my own fear of flying—and that was a pretty big fear."

"But it is also a big dream of yours, isn't it? To travel? And from what you've said, it sounds like Thomas is supportive of that. Bella, I don't mean to get in your business. It's just that I've learned so much traveling on my own these last months. I think you'd surprise yourself and I know you could handle it. And what with your writing and what you've told me about your future plans—"

"Sorry. I know what you're saying. It does make sense, but I really can't imagine it on my own—at least not right now. And things between Thomas and me are so new—well, the status change, that is—not our relationship. But I just feel like we need to get a solid foundation under us, you know?"

Nina was looking at her intently.

"What, Nina?"

"Look, I know it's none of my business."

"But?"

"But it sure seems that you and Thomas have a very solid basis for your relationship—one that's based on true friendship. You can't ask for more than that, I think."

"Okay...and?"

"And I'd just hate for you to give up on your own dreams, that's all."

"You sound like Thomas."

"He's a good man." Nina winked at her.

"Yes, that he is. Oh, I can't really think about anything else right now but our upcoming trip to New York. I'm sure everything will be fine and also nothing is set in stone, right? Isn't that what you told me the other day?" Isabella laughed lightly but truly did want the conversation to end.

"Yes, it's one of the biggest things I've learned while on my travels—and through my divorce, really, although I suppose that's a pretty negative way to look at marriage. So don't base your early lovely relationship on any mottos that you've learned from me." It was Nina's turn to laugh.

Isabella leaned over to hug her friend. "Well, I'm not going to say that I'm sad for you because you seem pretty happy right now, and all this relationship stuff is really new for me. So, I guess I have a lot to learn about love and trust. Well, I've always felt that way about Thomas, but you know what I mean. It's like a whole new level of feelings for me."

"Yes, Bella. I know. And I know you're going to figure everything out for yourself, whether you decide to settle down in the city or head back out for new adventures. You're so young and you've obviously got the means to live however you choose to. I envy your youth." Nina reached out to squeeze Isabella's hand. "So I guess I'm just trying to give you the advice that I wish someone had given me when I rushed into everything so quickly with my ex. I had plenty of dreams that I just shoved to the side back then— things that I didn't even let myself think about for the past ten years—and I do regret that lost time."

"But you're doing those things now and that's what matters."

"Yes, you're right." Nina smiled as she stood up. "And now it's definitely time for me to stay out of your business. But you know I'm only a video chat away if you need to talk at any time."

Isabella stood up from the bench and reached over to give Nina a hug. "I do know that, and thank you. Meeting you has definitely been one of the highlights of all my travels so far. And I will think about everything that you've shared with me. Promise. Now shall we finish our hike so that we can reward ourselves with coffee?"

"Sounds like a plan to me," said Nina.

SIX

Isabella looked up at Thomas as he burst in the door, threw his backpack down on the sofa, and grabbed a can of Coke from the kitchen fridge, all in what seemed like the same second. He sat down on the sofa as he took a long drink and finally looked over to where Isabella sat on the floor amidst the various pieces of a shelf that she'd been trying unsuccessfully to put together for the past thirty minutes.

"Iz, what are you doing? I told you I'd put that together over the weekend."

"No, actually that was last week that you said that." Isabella laughed lightly as she got up to sit beside him on the sofa, leaning over to give him a slight hug as she did so. "I'm just getting kind of tired of looking at all the boxes in here, so I thought I'd give it a shot myself—something I might actually regret now." She sighed and tucked her legs under her.

Thomas laughed and took one more big swig of soda before setting the empty can down on the coffee table. He looked over at her, then grabbed her hands to pull her to him as he stretched out. "What's that look for?"

"What look?"

"The look that says you've got something to say." Thomas laughed and tugged on her hair lightly. "Spill it."

"Well, for one thing, I thought you were trying to cut back on the soda..."

"Alright, Mom." Thomas laughed but it seemed slightly strained, and Isabella felt his body tense just a little beside her as he spoke.

"Oh, come on. You're the one that said you wanted to cut back on your caffeine. So, I'm only thinking of you, my darling." Isabella kissed him playfully on the nose, hoping it was enough to lighten the slightly uncomfortable mood in the room.

"I know. You're right. But it's all I can do to stay awake for my afternoon classes if I don't get at least one in before noon."

"Well, if you'd go to bed earlier, then you might not have that problem." As soon as the words were out of her mouth, she regretted them. She'd been doing that a lot lately and she felt her stomach tense just thinking about it.

"Really, Iz?" Thomas pushed her off him slightly as he sat up. "Look, I think things are going to calm down a bit, but it's only been two weeks since classes started. Give me a break, would ya?" He laughed lightly, but it sounded forced to Isabella and she felt like she'd been punched in the gut.

"I know. I'm sorry, Thomas. I didn't mean it." She tried to hold back the tears as she leaned in to kiss his cheek. "You're right, and I'm horrible for even bugging you about stuff. You're doing great and I'm so proud of you."

Thomas pulled his leg up on the sofa as he grabbed her hands, shifting his body slightly so that they were facing one another. "You're not horrible." He leaned in to give her a quick kiss on the lips. "You're lovely, adorable, and slightly neurotic." Thomas laughed and Isabella punched him playfully on the arm. "But Iz, you knew that there was going to be an adjustment period here for me. This is what I tried to tell you and also why I wasn't sure that your coming here was the best idea."

Isabella felt her stomach drop at his words, which were all true. She wasn't doing a good job supporting him. She knew better than to complain after all the discussions that the two of them had had about how important it was to Thomas to start out on the right foot when it came to his classes and his studies. She'd vowed to be supportive, yet all she seemed to be noticing was the time that Thomas didn't have for her ever since his classes had started. She tried to force a smile as she looked at him now.

"I know. You're right. I think I just need to get busier myself. I need more things to occupy my time."

"Well, on that note, did you see that apartment this morning? The one you were telling me about in SoHo?"

Isabella wrinkled her nose. "No. It's too far."

"Iz, it's not too far. It's a fifteen-minute cab ride—thirty minutes tops with traffic." Thomas nudged her lightly in her side. "I think it would be helpful to you to get settled and know where you're going to be—for your writing, I mean."

"It would be better for you if I moved out, wouldn't it?" Isabella held her breath as she waited for him to answer. Why was she making everything so miserable for him? She sounded like a nagging annoying girlfriend, which was the last thing she wanted to be.

Thomas was shaking his head. "That's not fair. You know that you can live here. But—"

"But what?" *Just shut up, Isabella. You're going to push him away.*

"Well, that's not what you want. Is it? I'm only going by what we've talked about before and honestly, Iz, I'm just afraid that my not being around very much is going to continue to bug you. I'm not sure how to make that better—at least for now. I just think that the sooner you can feel settled and get into your own routine, the better. For you, I mean."

Isabella nodded her head and then stood up from the sofa. "No, you're right. I'm being ridiculous. I'm sorry, Thomas. I know that you have enough on your mind without having to worry about me too. I'm sure I'll find a place soon. The realtor e-mailed me with a few other options this morning, actually."

Thomas stood up and pulled her to him in a hug. "You're not being ridiculous. We're just talking things through, right? 'Cuz that's what healthy couples do." He winked at her and then walked across the room to where the pieces of shelving still lay strewn about the floor. "So, I have about thirty minutes before I need to leave for my next class. Shall we see if we can get this shelf put together before I go?"

Isabella smiled, feeling much better than she had even a few minutes earlier. "How 'bout if I go fix you some lunch while you get started on that? Maybe a sandwich and a small salad?"

"Yes, please. That would be great."

"I think that shelf looks great. What do you think?" Thomas took a big bite of his sandwich and looked across the table past Isabella to the shelf that now stood against the wall.

"Perfect. Now I can unpack your last boxes of books for you. We just need to find the table for the dining room and then I think you'll be all set."

"Oh, sorry. I meant to tell you. I found one the other day in between classes—at a shop uptown. I gotta double-check but I think they are supposed to be delivering it this afternoon around two. I should have checked with you to make sure you were going to be here, though. Does that work? Or I can call them to arrange another time."

"This afternoon is fine. I'm also expecting something from Lia. According to the tracking, I should be getting it this afternoon too, so I can hang out here, no problem."

"Oh yeah? What is Lia sending you?"

Isabella smiled as she thought about her grandmother and the conversation that they'd had the day before. Ever since Isabella had left Tuscany with Thomas after Christmas, they'd done a great job of keeping in touch with one another. And she missed Lia and her grandfather. She missed them all—Jemma, Blu, Gigi, Douglas, and all the kids. Christmas had been really special for Isabella, and she vowed not to go very long in between visits now that this wonderful new extended family existed in her life.

She turned her attention back to Thomas, who was giving her a little kick under the table. "Oh, sorry. I don't know exactly what Lia sent me. She said that a few days ago she was clearing out some boxes in the attic and she ran across something of Arianna's that was meant for me."

"Ooh, that sounds exciting." Thomas grinned.

"It does, doesn't it?"

Isabella had actually been pretty consumed thinking about what the item might be. She kept everything of her birth mother's in a box that now resided inside Thomas's closet. The pictures, journals, locket and, of course, the map. She would put it up again just as soon as she was settled. Thinking about the map reminded her of her birth mother's ashes, also kept in a small urn within the leather box. She'd gotten a good start at spreading them, but she knew the map would taunt her until the ashes were all gone.

"Well, text me a picture when it arrives—your surprise, I mean —not the table." Thomas stood up from the table and walked over to get his backpack from the sofa. "I gotta run. Thanks for lunch, Iz."

Isabella got up too and made her way to where he stood so that she could give him a hug goodbye. "So, are you coming home before dinner or will you be meeting us at the restaurant tonight?"

Thomas looked like a deer caught in headlights. "Uh—sorry, what's tonight?"

"Thomas—my parents. Remember? Please tell me you didn't forget. They're only here one more night."

"Oh man. I'm sorry, Iz. I did forget, and I do have an important study group tonight—for that big test I have tomorrow. Do you think your parents will understand?"

For what felt like the hundredth time that day, Isabella tried to hold back sudden tears that threatened. Her parents would understand but Thomas's forgetfulness wasn't making her feel any better about things.

She followed him to the door and attempted a smile as he kissed her on the cheek. "Yeah, I'm sure they will. Don't worry about it."

"Well, text me the address and I'll do my best to be there for dessert, okay?" He leaned forward to kiss her on the forehead. "And I am sorry that I forgot."

"It's okay. You better get going. Have a good afternoon."

"You're the best. Love you, babe."

"I love you too."

Isabella shut the door and then burst into tears.

SEVEN

Isabella sat at the new dining table holding the small package in her hands. She turned the box over to read her grandmother's careful handwriting on the outside, before peeling back the closure to reveal the contents. She reached her hand in to first pull out a beautiful homemade card with a picture of her grandparents' vineyard on the outside.

Isabella smiled as she admired the colors of the sunrise and noticed that she'd memorized the details of the landscape where they lived. She'd always been taken with the idea of visiting Italy. It had been at the top of a list that had seemed nearly impossible back when she'd had an intense fear of flying. Yet, by some crazy miracle, Tuscany was where she'd landed. And Tuscany, along with her family that she'd met there, had been magical.

And it was where Thomas had told her that he loved her for the first time—where he'd told Isabella that he was *in* love with her.

She opened the card to find the letter from Lia inside.

Dearest Isabella,

. . .

I still miss you every day that you're not here but your grandfather and I are thankful for every day that we have the chance to get to know you more. I hope that you will come back soon, and please do bring that lovely boyfriend of yours around again. You are both always welcome here.

While I was sorting through some boxes in the attic the other day, I came upon this journal of your mother's. Somehow it got separated from the rest of Arianna's things and I wanted you to have it right away. I've not read it. Just as I'd saved the others she'd set aside for you, this one also is for your eyes only.

As always, I hope that the contents will help you to know her that much more.

We hope that you are feeling settled and happy in New York City.

We love you, Bella.
Lia and Antonio

Isabella grinned as she read the words from her grandmother. She could hear her voice—with the lovely slight Italian accent—as she read the words, and it instantly took her back to Italy in her mind.

How easy would it be for her to pack up and head back there to spend time at the vineyard? Isabella shocked herself as the thought struck her. No. They'd decided—she and Thomas—that she was going to give New York a try. She wouldn't go back to Tuscany until Thomas could join her during the summer. And summer in Tuscany would be beautiful.

She tipped the box slightly to allow the journal to fall out lightly on the table. It was unlike most of the others, in that it was a lovely leather journal, mustard yellow in color and only slightly worn at its edges. There had been a few nicer journals from the latter years of Arianna's life, but many of the ones that Isabella now possessed were spiral-bound notebooks that her birth mother had kept as diaries throughout her younger years—writing down her thoughts long before she knew that her life would be cut so short.

Isabella had loved reading them all, getting to know her mother through her words on the worn pages. Through reading Arianna's journals, Isabella had come to know a young girl who'd had many of the same fears and insecurities that she herself had experienced during those same critical years in her life. She loved all the journals, but the ones that were written after Arianna had become pregnant with her were the ones that Isabella had spent hours poring over.

It meant everything to her to know every detail that Arianna had written about her daughter growing inside her. The anger and the angst that made Isabella weep only made her feel more connected to a mother that she'd never had the chance to know. Arianna *had* wanted her. Every doubt that Isabella had ever had in regards to the imagined circumstances of her birth was erased the moment that she'd read those journals.

Of everything that Arianna had left Isabella—and she'd left her a lot—it was the journals that by far meant the most to her. She treasured them and would never tire of reading her mother's words to her.

Isabella carefully opened the journal to read the inside label. Arianna had written the dates inside every cover of every journal. She felt her heart beating faster when she read what was written inside this one.

Final journal of Arianna Sinclair

When Isabella had read the last journal of the ones she already had, she'd thought that it ended rather abruptly. In it, Arianna had been writing to her at that point and Isabella assumed that she'd had to stop because of her illness—because of the fact that she'd grown too weak to find the words or the energy to write them down as she faced her final days. But this journal seemed to tell a different story, and Isabella felt the tears already stinging her eyes as she carried it across the room to settle in with it on the more comfortable sofa.

She leafed through the pages, delighted to find that every one had been written on. Some appeared to be Arianna's own thoughts written for herself, many others were addressed to her— addressed to Arianna's daughter.

She opened the journal to the first page, a page that had been written just for Isabella.

Dearest Daughter,

By now you've read so many words that I've written over the years, many of which I'm sure have bored you to tears. Others I hope have inspired you, but mostly I hope they've helped you to let go of any anger that you might have.

I know about hanging on to anger, Bella.

Isabella grinned at the name—what Arianna had decided to call her daughter, without ever having known the name that Isabella had been given by her adoptive parents. It was just another of the many signs that made Isabella feel that much more connected to Arianna.

She brought her attention back to the journal as she continued reading.

I'm sure that you are far better than I've been about letting go of your anger. I'm confident that you are not the type to hang on to some-

thing that will not serve you in any positive way. And I've let my anger go, but I wish that my own mother would have known my forgiveness before her accident. I am choosing to believe that you have forgiven me by now—not for me, but for you, dear one.

So I wanted to let you know how thankful I am for your forgiveness. I don't take it or your understanding lightly. I only wish I could hold you in my arms as I weep with the full acceptance of it.

Isabella continued to read, thumbing through page after page that allowed her more glimpses into her birth mother's final days. There were several letters written to Isabella, but there were also lists and pages that Arianna had written to seemingly gather her own thoughts as her body and mind grew more weary with her illness during those last days.

Isabella's breath caught slightly as she turned a page and read the heading.

Things I Regret

It was an unusual thing for her to come across, because most of Arianna's words were about not having regrets and the things that she'd made peace with during those last days of her life. But this seemed different. Isabella bit into her bottom lip as she scanned the list, imagining the emotion behind each item that a young girl faced with death might be feeling.

- I regret not having the chance to tell my parents that I loved them before their accident. Especially my mother, who most likely died without ever having known my forgiveness or how much I truly loved her despite our differences.

- I regret the way I handled things with Lucas. He deserved to know that he had a daughter and I should have fought harder to share the truth with him.

. . .

Isabella smiled as she read the mention of her birth father's name. *It's okay, Arianna. Lucas forgives you and we are family now.* There was so much that Arianna would never know. Isabella wiped away a tear as she continued reading.

- I will never regret the trip to Italy with Lia. Those were the best days of my life. But I do regret that I didn't get to see the world. I regret that I didn't get the chance to travel on my own—to discover those things about myself that can only be discovered from being out of my comfort zone. I regret that I didn't take more chances and allow myself to feel the fear of the unknown just a little bit more often.

Isabella reread Arianna's words two more times before she closed the journal, walked over to get her laptop, and smiled as she pulled up her favorite travel-booking site.

EIGHT

Isabella hummed along to the song that played from her laptop as she folded the last of the clothes to go in her suitcase. It was late, but she wasn't tired and she wanted to talk to Thomas when he got home.

He'd texted her earlier while she'd been out to dinner with her parents, apologizing that he wouldn't be able to make it—that he'd see Isabella at the apartment later. She'd been disappointed but there'd been so much on her mind—so much to discuss with her parents—that she thought it was actually for the best.

She looked up as she heard the sound of the door opening.

"Hi, babe. Sorry it's so late. The study group was good for me, though. I think I'm going to ace this test tomorrow." Thomas put his backpack down and crossed the room to where Isabella stood, kissing her on the cheek.

Isabella saw his eyes take in her suitcase through the open door of the bedroom as she reached up to give him a hug. "That's great about the study group."

Thomas stepped around her and just into the bedroom. "Did you take an apartment, Iz?"

"Nope. I guess I have some news for you." Isabella laughed lightly as Thomas turned around with a look of confusion on his face.

"You're not leaving me, are you? Because I'm not going to let you go so easily, you know." He laughed as he grabbed her up into his arms and sat down on the sofa with her on his lap.

Isabella snuggled against him, before she kissed him on the lips. "Is that so?"

He kissed her back and then looked her in the eyes intently. "It is. Yes. So, you gonna tell me what's up?"

"Well, the bad news—for you—is that I *am* leaving you." She laughed lightly. "But the good news is that I'm not *leaving* you leaving you."

"Meaning, wherever it is you're going, you're still my girl?"

Thomas kissed the tip of her nose, and Isabella felt her heartbeat quicken as it still did sometimes during those moments when she realized that Thomas was her boyfriend now.

She pulled away slightly so that she could look at him. "I'm still your girl, yes. I'll always be your girl, mister—well, as long as you'll have me."

"So forever then. It's settled."

There was that look in his eyes—the one that made Isabella forget everything else and the one that was nearly causing her to second-guess the decision she'd made just hours earlier.

Isabella's thoughts swirled as Thomas kissed her deeply, and she realized that leaving him might be the worst mistake she'd ever make.

But in the next moment, she remembered Arianna's words that she'd read, that had spoken so clearly to her, and she knew that she wouldn't change her mind. She slid off Thomas's lap and onto the sofa next to him, taking his hand in hers as she did so.

"I booked a flight to Thailand. I leave tomorrow—in the evening." She felt her heart race just thinking about what she'd done so spontaneously.

Thomas squeezed her hand and grinned at her. "Really, Iz? That's fantastic."

"It is?" She laughed but the laugh was nervous now. Was she really going to get on a plane to Thailand tomorrow all by herself?

"Well, I think so. And you must think so too, at least a little bit. What made you change your mind? I'm excited for you. But Iz..."

"Yeah?"

"I hope you're not leaving because of me—because of anything I've said or done to make you feel unwelcome here. That's the last thing I'd want, honey."

Isabella looked at the concern on his face, thankful for the way that Thomas always thought about her feelings. "No. No, it has nothing to do with you or me being here, really. I got the package from Lia today." She smiled. "It was a misplaced journal of Arianna's—the last one she'd written, actually."

"Ah. I see. What a wonderful surprise for you. Wanna tell me about it?" Thomas shifted his body on the sofa so that it was easier for them to talk.

"I'll share it all with you at some point. For now, let's just say that I read something there that made me feel connected to her once again in regards to the travel—something that made me think that staying here now is not the right thing for me at this time. You were right when you said that I shouldn't cut my travels early to come back. As much as I hate the idea of leaving you—" Isabella's voice broke and the tears started to fall.

"Shh." Thomas leaned in to gently wipe away her tears with his fingertips and pull her toward him for a big hug. "You're not leaving me. You're going toward something wonderful. I'm not going anywhere—well, unless it's to somewhere exotic to meet you for Christmas." He sat back so that he could look at her. "How long are you planning to be gone, by the way?"

Isabella laughed through her tears, which had continued to

fall. "I don't know. Thomas? Would you really come visit—if I stay away that long?"

"Are you kidding? Of course I will. Well, assuming there's nothing crazy happening around here with school, I mean." He took her hand in his, gently rubbing it as he continued. "Iz, don't think for one moment that watching you go will be an easy thing for me. I'm going to miss you like crazy. You do know that, don't you?"

For the first time in a long time, Isabella felt such peace wash over her. She was so very thankful for this incredible man in her life. She nodded her head as he waited for her response. "Yes, I think I do know that now. Thank you for telling me, though. I love you so much. Oh, I know I'm going to miss you every second."

"Well, that just means that our reunion is going to be quite sweet, I'd imagine." Thomas wiggled his eyebrows, which made Isabella burst out laughing.

"I'd imagine that you might be right about that."

Thomas's face grew more serious. "I just want to say that I think it's wonderful that you seem to have this incredible connection with your birth mother—about the travel, but everything really. When I think about all that's happened since you found out about Arianna—well, it's just been really good for you, Iz. I think it's made you more confident—more of the person you're meant to be—more Izzy goodness for me to love."

Isabella laughed, loving the words that Thomas had chosen. "Thank you—for saying that. It means a lot to me."

Thomas hugged her close. "Now, I think we better get some sleep. Well, I better get to bed if I have any hope of doing a decent job at my ten o'clock exam tomorrow. I'm thinking maybe after my test, I'll skip the afternoon classes so that we can spend the day together before you leave. If that works for you?" He grinned.

"Really? That sounds perfect. I'll finish my packing in the morning and I'll be all yours from lunch on then."

"It's a date." Thomas kissed her on the lips. "Good night, love."

"Night, Thomas." Isabella grinned, the happiness and love she was feeling overshadowing any doubts she had about leaving the next day—for the moment, anyway.

NINE

Isabella lowered her seat back and looked out the window of the plane. It still hadn't completely sunk in that she was on her way to Thailand—a place as foreign and exotic to her as any she could have picked. At Nina's earlier suggestion, she'd decided to skip the craziness of big-city Bangkok, opting instead to fly straight into the smaller city of Chiang Mai in the north. Nina had said that it was a place that she herself could settle down in for months, and she just knew that it was the best starting point for Isabella in terms of her Southeast Asia travels.

Isabella couldn't wait to talk to Nina. She hadn't told her yet about her travels. Everything had happened so quickly that she'd decided to surprise her friend with a video chat after she was settled in her new home for the next few weeks.

Isabella was proud of herself in regards to the little bit of planning that she'd done. She'd found what looked like a great apartment in the neighborhood where Nina had lived. Because she'd decided to travel so last-minute, there'd been no time to get a visa, so she'd have the thirty days upon arrival. After that, she'd see how she felt about everything. And if it didn't feel right, she could always go back to New York—back to Thomas.

Thomas.

She closed her eyes as she thought about the day they'd had together. He'd come home straight after his exam to take her to her favorite lunch spot, followed by a walk in Central Park. He'd seemed relaxed to her—more like himself than he had since school had started. They'd laughed, kissed, and enjoyed the entire afternoon together before it was time to take the taxi to the airport.

He'd been so sweet to her, making it nearly impossible for her to actually say goodbye to him at the airport. She'd cried until she didn't think she had any tears left, but Thomas had brushed them aside, assuring her that he could come to see her over the holiday break regardless of where she was at that time.

The thought was reassuring. Three months. That's how long it would be until she saw him again—if she stayed away for that long. She could handle it. And somewhere deep down inside she knew that she could more than handle it.

The next three months were going to be about her again— about stretching herself to find out more about who she was and the things that she wanted. And she planned to really get into a good routine with her writing—to plan out her next series and figure out what her goals were in terms of her writing career. She'd let things slide recently with all of the pressure of moving and getting settled, and she was determined to get back to something that she'd loved her entire life.

Thinking about her writing reminded her that she needed to call Jemma as soon as she was settled. Her friend had been such a cheerleader to her when she'd been working on her first book, and Isabella missed her dearly. They'd exchanged quick texts about Isabella's travels, but the two hadn't had a chance to really talk since Isabella had left Greece. She had a lot to tell her friend and she also needed to find out how everything was going with her and Rafael in Guatemala. It was funny to her that only a few short months ago, she and Jemma had been traveling together throughout Europe. It reminded her how quickly things could change. And for some reason, this thought about things changing caused a little flutter in the pit of her stomach.

She wanted change but she didn't want things to change between her and Thomas. That was her greatest fear. But could she learn to let the fear go? To just accept things as they were—as they should be?

She sighed as she took one last look out the window before closing her eyes. She needed some sleep if she was going to tackle this adventure ahead with clear thoughts and an open mind.

Isabella lifted the shade of her window at the instruction of the flight attendant. It had been a long journey with a layover in Shanghai—over twenty-four hours since she'd said goodbye to Thomas—and she was ready to be off the plane.

She watched out her window as the plane made its descent and the loveliness of Chiang Mai was spread out below her for the first time. It nearly took her breath away as she realized how small the airport was and that it appeared tucked into the beautiful hills that surrounded it.

She reached for her purse and checked the instructions that she'd written down from what she'd researched online. Everything seemed pretty straightforward. Go through passport control, collect her bags, go through the final check, stop at the ATM machine to get Thai baht and then on to the taxi stand.

She bit her bottom lip and felt the butterflies in her stomach as the airplane came to its final stop and the passengers stood to stretch and collect their belongings. *You can do this, Isabella. Just follow the instructions.*

At the same moment as she felt the fear of the unknown for what was ahead, she smiled as she thought about the fact that she'd had zero fear about the actual flight. Yes, she *had* been conquering some big fears this past year. She was determined to keep reminding herself of that.

She practically could have ticked each item off a checklist, it had been that easy to get through customs and collect her bags. She had her money all sorted and was only waiting for the taxi that she'd paid for inside.

She took a deep breath in and noticed all of the smiling faces surrounding her. There were plenty of foreigners, but interspersed with the English that she heard was the distinct sound of what could only be Thai. She had only taken the time to download a language app to her phone, but she hoped that she could at least pick up a few phrases while she was here.

"Hi, is this your first time to Chiang Mai?"

The voice from behind startled her—so much so that she jumped a little as she turned around.

"Oh, sorry. I didn't mean to startle you."

She smiled at the man who'd spoken to her. "Oh, no worries at all. I guess I was a little zoned out there—travel brain." She laughed. "And yes, it is my first time to Chiang Mai—first time to Thailand and to Asia, for that matter. And you?"

"I've been living here for the past year—just in from a visa run." He put his bag down and extended his hand to her. "I'm Dylan, by the way."

Isabella reached out to take his hand. "Nice to meet you. I'm Is —I'm Bella." Using her new nickname seemed fitting for her new surroundings.

Dylan grinned widely at her. "Well, it's nice to meet you, Bella. Hey, I'm happy to show you around if you like. I know it can all be a bit overwhelming when you first arrive."

She felt herself tense up for a second, but then immediately relaxed when she saw his expression. Dylan was kind. She could sense it, and she wanted to trust her gut about people on this trip. "Really? That's so nice of you. I'd love it, actually. Maybe tomorrow, after I've had a chance to get some sleep?"

"Yes, sure. Let me give you my card. My e-mail address is on there and my Thai phone number, which you probably won't be able to use yet, but I can help you with all that too—if you want to get a local number. E-mail me later, but I will plan to be all yours tomorrow."

Isabella felt herself grinning widely as the taxi pulled up beside her. "I'll do that—just as soon as I check into my apartment and figure out the wi-fi. Thanks again—so much. It was great meeting you, Dylan."

"You too, Bella. Enjoy your first afternoon in Chiang Mai. Oh, if you have the chance and are hungry, get yourself some Khao Soi."

"Super. Thanks for that recommendation. I'll see you tomorrow."

Isabella got into the taxi and confirmed that the driver knew where they were headed. She looked down at Dylan's card still in her hand.

Dylan Black
Best-Selling Thriller Author

He's a writer. Isabella smiled. Yes, she was going to learn to trust her instincts—to trust herself—on this trip.

TEN

Isabella opened her eyes, forgetting for a moment where she was. She reached for her phone on the nightstand. 8:00. Was that a.m. or p.m.? U.S. time or Thailand time? It had been three o'clock in the afternoon when her taxi driver had dropped her off at her apartment. Had she slept through the night?

She climbed out of bed to make her way over to the window, where she could see that it was dark out. It was night, and that also explained why she suddenly felt famished. She went into the bathroom to check her face and put her hair up in a ponytail. Should she change out of her jeans? It had felt extremely hot even for the little bit that she'd been outside at the airport.

She rummaged around in her suitcase for a casual skirt to change into, grabbed her purse, and headed down to the lobby. After getting a map and what seemed like easy directions from the woman at reception, she walked outside in search of her first authentic Thai meal in Thailand. The woman had told her to walk two blocks up and turn right—that this would be the main road where she'd find tons of restaurants, cafes, shops, massages, and anything else she might need.

When she'd chosen the apartment, the location had been a big factor for her, so as she made the turn onto the busier street, she was quite pleased at how accurate the description had been. Everywhere she looked, there was something new and fascinating to see. The sidewalks were bustling with foreigners and Thais. People said hello to her as she passed by the shops.

She slowed down outside what looked like a small massage parlor and just as soon as she'd stopped for a second, a small Thai woman came outside to greet her.

"Excuse me, miss. Do you want massage? I give you good rate. Only two hundred baht. One hour."

Isabella smiled as she took out her phone to check her currency app. Six dollars. Could that be right? Nina had told her about the wonderful Thai massages that she could get, but six dollars seemed too incredible to be real.

She turned to the woman, who was waiting patiently by the door. "Maybe I'll come back tomorrow. Right now I need to find some food."

The woman grinned and patted Isabella on the back. "No problem, miss. You go eat good Thai food. Everything here delicious. Go see my cousin. Two more streets. Right side. Called Thai House. Very good food—best in Chiang Mai."

Isabella smiled back at her. "I will do that. Thank you."

She continued up the street, soaking in the sights and sounds. She passed several bars with live music and tables filled with people who seemed to be having a good time. There were street carts selling different types of skewered meats and vegetables. On the back of a pickup, there was a guy grilling something while a line of people waited.

When she came to the spot where the restaurant should be, she didn't see anything obvious right away. There were several bigger restaurants that seemed to have plenty of seating available. There were only tourists or westerners seated inside, from what Isabella could make out.

She continued walking past, thinking that if she didn't see the other place before the end of the block, she'd come back, as she really was beyond hungry at this point. No sooner had she passed the bigger restaurants than she came upon a smaller one that was bursting with local people—all laughing and eating what looked and smelled like the most delicious food she'd ever seen. Sure enough, on the window she could barely make out the name of the restaurant.

Thai House

Open

She tentatively stepped just inside the door to be greeted just as quickly by a man in an apron. "Come in, please, miss. Sit down."

Isabella's eyes darted around the crowded space, quickly realizing that there were no open tables. "Oh, I can wait for a table. You are very busy." She smiled.

"No, no. Come in, please sit." The man gestured to a large round table where Isabella could see that there was only one empty chair among the many that were already occupied.

A woman seated at the table, with one child sitting on her lap and another next to her, grinned at Isabella and pointed to the chair. "Sit. Please."

Isabella made her way over to the table. "Are you sure?"

"Yes. Please."

Isabella sat down on the small chair and looked at the little boy seated next to her, who'd been watching her with wide eyes.

"Hello." She grinned at him, thinking how adorable the two children were.

She didn't miss the little nudge to the back that his mother gave him right before he put his hands together and bowed his head. "*Sah wah dee khrap.*"

Isabella had done just enough of a quick study of Thailand to recognize the Thai greeting along with the wai—the slight bow with the palms together. From the looks of things, it seemed to be as she'd read—that children learned this at a very early age as a sign of respect. She took a deep breath and decided that it was as good a time as any to try her first Thai phrase.

She looked over at the mother. "*Sah wah dee khrap.*"

The mother smiled politely, but the little boy burst out laughing as he said something to his mother, who knocked him lightly on the head in a scolding way.

Isabella laughed lightly. "Did I say it wrong? Please teach me the correct way."

The woman smiled at her. "You say, *sah wah dee khaa*. No *khrap*."

"Only boys say *khrap*. Girls only say *khaa*," the little boy interrupted, his eyes wide again.

The woman nodded her head. "Yes, we say *sah wah dee khaa*. Men say *sah wah dee khrap*."

"Oh...*sah wah dee khaa*. Is that better?" She smiled at the little boy, who was nodding his head. "It means hello?" she asked the mother.

"Yes. It is our greeting."

"Thank you."

"You say, *korb kun khaa*." She smiled at Isabella. "This means thank you."

"*Korb kun khaa*—for teaching me my first Thai words."

They smiled at one another and the man with the apron came over to hand Isabella a menu. She looked down at it and laughed. "No English?"

"No, sorry."

The woman sitting beside her handed the toddler in her lap to the woman on the other side of her. "Here. I will help you. What do you like? Do you eat meat?"

Isabella laughed. "Oh, your English is very good. Thank you— I mean, *korb kun khaa*. Yes, I do eat meat. Maybe something with chicken?"

Isabella spent a good ninety minutes or more chatting with her new Thai friends and drawing funny characters for the little boy, who'd brought out paper and crayons midway through her conversation with his mother. He seemed to think Isabella was hilarious and delighted in drawing her items that he could then teach her the Thai word for.

By the time Isabella's food came, she'd already been having the most delightful night. As the waiter set several dishes of food in front of her, she laughed and invited everyone at the table to dig in and help her. Everything was delicious. Several dishes were more spicy than she'd imagined, and her new friend quickly taught her how to ask for food with less spice—for next time, she'd said.

The owner of the restaurant brought her a Thai beer—on the house, he'd said—"to welcome our new friend to Chiang Mai"— and Isabella couldn't have asked for a better first night in her new home.

Finally, yawning and shocking herself that she could be tired after the big nap she'd had earlier that afternoon, she said goodbye to her new friends, promising to return again soon.

Just as she was getting up to leave, the little boy whispered something into his mother's ear, and she nodded. He ran over to Isabella with his hands outstretched and one of his drawings in his hand. "Miss, for you." He grinned widely.

"Oh. It's so beautiful. Thank—*korb kun khaa*, I mean." She bent down to hug the giggling child, who than ran back to his mother.

Isabella walked back out onto the sidewalk, feeling completely happy and at peace. She looked at the time on her phone. 10:30. She checked her world clock app to see that it was only late afternoon in Italy. If she could manage to stay awake long enough, she'd try to video message Nina. She was dying to talk to her friend—to surprise her with the news of where she was.

Nina was going to be shocked.

Isabella smiled as she made her way back to her apartment,

stopping just long enough to get some delicious-looking mango sticky rice from a street vendor. Everything already felt so different here in Thailand, and so far she was loving every minute of it.

ELEVEN

Isabella settled onto the comfy sofa with her laptop. So far, she was feeling quite pleased with her apartment. It was well equipped with a small kitchen, two bedrooms, two baths, and a lovely living room with a desk by a window that looked out toward the mountain, Doi Suthep. She'd read about the temple there and had noticed earlier that she could see it from her window. She also had a big balcony outside of the living room that had the same gorgeous view. Yes, she'd done a good job choosing the place where she'd be living for at least the next month. She had the feeling that she'd be feeling quite inspired to write from her sweet little desk with a view.

She reached into her purse to get the piece of paper with the wi-fi code that had been given to her earlier when she'd checked in. She pulled it out along with the business card that Dylan had given her at the airport. She'd send him a quick e-mail before she tried to call Nina.

She sent the e-mail off, suggesting to Dylan that they meet any time after ten the next morning, depending on what would work best for him. Remarkably, she was feeling pretty tired again so she had high hopes of sleeping through the night despite the potential jet lag that she'd only somewhat prepared herself for. If she woke up early, she'd use that time to catch up on her writing. She'd always preferred to write in the early mornings anyway, so it wouldn't be a bad habit to start again.

Isabella smiled as she turned on her video chat and clicked on Nina's profile to attempt to connect with her. The two had last chatted on video shortly after Isabella had arrived in New York. Nina had been renting a room at a beautiful villa outside of Florence and she'd looked happy and relaxed.

Isabella, on the other hand, had felt stressed out when they'd last spoken. She and Thomas had been rushing around the city trying to find furniture and everything he needed before starting his classes. Their whole first week in New York had been a blur.

She smiled thinking about how quickly things could change. It was unbelievable to her that she was now calling Nina—only a few weeks later—from Thailand.

One ring, two, three, four. She was just about to give up and send Nina an e-mail instead, when her friend's smiling face filled the screen in front of her.

"Bella! What a nice surprise. You just caught me on my way out."

"Nina, it's so nice to see you. We can chat later if it's not a good time for you..."

"No, no. He can wait a few minutes more for me." Nina's grin was big and she looked completely happy.

"Wait. He? Who's he? Do tell."

"Oh, no. Not much to tell. Just a lovely Spanish man who's staying in the villa here. I'll tell you more later—*if* there is anything to tell after tonight, that it." She laughed. "But I want to hear about you. How is New York and how are you doing?"

"Well, I have some news myself." Isabella knew that she was grinning ear to ear as she paused for dramatic effect.

"Okay. Well, don't leave me hanging, girl." Nina laughed.

"You'll never guess where I am."

"Hmmm, really? Well, last I heard from you, you were apartment hunting in the Big Apple, so I'd guess that you've found yourself some fancy-pants penthouse apartment with plenty of room for me when I come visit."

"Ooh, that does sound like fun. No, I'm no longer in New York, but I do have a spare bedroom where I am—here in Chiang Mai!"

"What? Are you kidding me, Bella? When—and how—did that happen? Oh, I'm so excited for you—and slightly jealous—well, not to say that I'm not loving Italy, of course." She laughed.

"I only just arrived here this afternoon. I still can't quite believe it myself. Everything happened so fast."

"So what exactly does this mean? Not to be nosy, but is everything okay with you and Thomas? I'm only asking because you seemed so set on your decision to be in New York with him."

"Oh, yes. Everything with Thomas was—is—great. And I think he'll come to visit me at Christmas if I'm still traveling, so that's all good. And would you believe that it was my birth mother—once again—who kind of caused this all to happen?"

Isabella had already shared the story about Arianna and her journals with Nina during their time together in Greece. She filled her friend in about the missing journal that she'd received only days ago and read her the entry that had spoken so clearly to her.

"Wow, Bella. That's pretty incredible. I'm so glad that you listened—to Arianna, but also to your own inner voice. I think there's a reason behind the timing of everything, and you got that journal exactly when you were meant to have it. I mean, thank goodness you hadn't just signed a lease on an apartment after all, right?"

"I know. That's what I was thinking. And—well, if I'm being honest, something wasn't sitting well with me about New York. I mean, of course I wanted it to work and I do believe I would have made it work, but it was really all about Thomas, you know? Not that he was pressuring me in any way at all. It was never that. Just my own fears, I guess."

"Do you know what it was that you were afraid of?"

Isabella instinctively looked away from the screen in front of her. Yes, she knew what it was that she was *still* afraid of.

"Sorry, I don't mean to get in your business."

"No. No, it's okay. I was just thinking for a minute. Trying to find the honest answer to your question."

"Which is?"

"I guess I've been afraid of losing him—that whole out of sight, out of mind thing. His life is so different from mine right now. I'm sure he's going to be meeting all kinds of women—of people—at school, and—well, I'm not so sure that he won't forget about what we have. Does that make sense?"

Nina was nodding her head and looking thoughtful. "It does, but it doesn't sound like the Thomas I met in Greece at all. Bella, he adores you. I honestly don't think you have anything to worry about. Is it harder when you are away from one another? Probably. I think it will require some work to keep in touch—to communicate. But I think if the two of you are committed, you can make it work. Or…"

Isabella didn't miss the strange look that crossed her friend's face. "Or what?"

"Well, or maybe something else will happen and one or both of you will discover that it's not the right time."

Isabella felt her face fall at Nina's words.

"Oh, don't go to a weird place because of anything I'm saying. It's just that you're both so young. That's all. And having the gift of a few years on you and also a failed marriage behind me, I just want to be sure that you get a chance to sow your wild oats, so to speak." Nina winked at her and laughed lightly.

"Oh, I don't think I need to be worried about that. No one interests me like Thomas does—no one ever has. And I hope it's the same for him."

"Bella, I'm sure you have nothing to worry about. And anyway, try not to let it color your experience in Thailand. Now tell me everything. What is your first impression of Chiang Mai? Do you love it?"

Isabella laughed at her friend's sudden exuberance and then proceeded to tell her all about her apartment, the area where she was staying, and the fun meal she'd had that night. While they were talking, she noticed an alert pop up on her phone that Dylan had responded to her e-mail.

"Oh, and I met what seems like a really nice guy at the airport. He offered to show me around town—tomorrow, actually, which is so cool. He's been living here for awhile, so I suspect that he will have lots of good recommendations for me."

"What's his name? It's a pretty small circle of expats there and I may have met him."

Isabella reached for his card that she'd set down on the coffee table in front of her. "Dylan Black."

"Dylan? The writer, yeah?"

"Yes, that's right. Do you know him? How funny."

"I wouldn't say that I know him well, but I remember meeting him at an expat meet-up in town." She grinned at Isabella. "He's cute, right?"

Isabella felt her face instantly go warm. "Oh, I don't know. Is he? I hadn't really noticed."

"Oh, okay." Nina laughed. "I'm sure everything is going to be perfectly platonic between you, so you don't have to act like he's not attractive."

Isabella laughed too. "Of course. Well, it's cool that you know who he is, anyway."

"He did seem like a really great guy, and how wonderful that he's a writer, Bella. I'm sure he can give you some great ideas about places to work around town if you want to get out of your apartment to write at all. Chiang Mai is great for having a lot of really good cafes with wi-fi. I think you're going to like that aspect."

"I think so too. Well, let's not keep that date of yours waiting." Isabella winked at her friend. "Now that I'm actually here, do you have any final tips or recommendations for me? Things I should do right away?"

"Yes! I do, in fact. Tomorrow, or as soon as you're able, go book a massage with a sweet woman called Fai. You'll find the place on soi 12, which I think is just a few blocks from where you're staying."

"What's *soi*?" Isabella laughed. "I have a lot to learn."

"Oh, sorry. *Soi* is just the Thai word for street, basically. The area where you are staying has street signs, so it's pretty easy to get around. So, yeah. Go book a ninety-minute massage with Fai and tell her hello from me. She's really wonderful and I have the feeling you could use a massage, Bella."

Isabella laughed. "Oh you think so? Great. I will do that for sure. If you think of anything else, e-mail me, okay?"

"Will do—and Bella?"

"Yeah?"

"Do take the time to really soak everything in there, okay? I have the feeling that it's going to be really good for you—something that you need right now in your life."

Isabella smiled. "I will. And thank you. Now you go enjoy your Spanish man."

Isabella laughed as she closed the chat and then picked up her phone to check the response from Dylan.

TWELVE

Isabella had responded to Dylan's e-mail the night before with her address and a meeting time of ten o'clock in her lobby. It wasn't typical of her to give strangers the address of where she was staying, but after finding out that Nina knew of him, it didn't strike her as odd and it seemed the most reasonable thing to do.

She'd gotten a good night's sleep and was feeling surprisingly well, despite the time change for her. After getting ready, she still had an hour until Dylan's arrival. She opened up her e-mail to check if there was anything from Thomas. They'd exchanged a few quick text messages after she'd arrived the day before, but it had been the middle of the night his time and he'd had classes the next morning, so she was dying to have a real chat with him.

She opened up her video chat when she realized it wasn't too late to try him. After a few rings, the application stopped connecting abruptly. He'd declined the incoming call. Isabella felt her body tense as she stared at her phone, waiting to get a message from him. Within seconds she received the incoming text.

Sorry, Iz. At a party and it's too loud to talk. Can we try tomorrow?

Why did she feel like she'd just been punched in the gut? He was at a party? College students went to parties. She couldn't expect him to just be sitting home waiting for her to call. She punched in a quick text back.

Sure. I can't wait to talk to you. I miss you, T. xo

I miss you more. Love u. xo

She smiled as she fired off one last text. He loved her. That's what mattered.

Love u too.

She responded to a few other e-mails and before she knew it, it was time to head downstairs to the lobby to meet Dylan.

Isabella saw Dylan enter the lobby just as she was exiting the elevator. She couldn't help being reminded of Nina's proclamation when she'd told her friend that she'd met Dylan. He *was* good-looking. She watched him for a few seconds before he noticed her walking toward where he stood looking out the window. He was tall and had dark curly hair—not tight curls, but the kind that looked like he'd just rolled out of bed and run his fingers through his hair.

He turned around as she came closer and she noticed first his eyes, then his wide smile. They were a brilliant shade of blue—almost as if he had to be wearing colored contact lenses, but Isabella would bet money on the fact that he wasn't. And now she really couldn't get Nina's statement out of her mind. But it was okay that she was spending the day with him, wasn't it? He was a new much-needed friend and Thomas wasn't the type to be jealous—not that there would be anything to be jealous of. Isabella shook her head as if doing so would stop the ridiculous thoughts she was now having.

"Bella, hi. It's so good to see you again." Dylan took a step toward her and kissed her on the cheek.

She smiled back at him. "It's good to see you too. Thanks so much for meeting me here. I hope it wasn't too out of the way for you."

"No. I actually live in the same neighborhood, only a few streets over from you. You did a great job choosing your location, by the way. This is one of the nicer apartment buildings for sure."

Isabella felt herself tense up a little bit. She still wasn't completely used to her new financial status and it was moments like this that she was reminded that she was able to afford a much different lifestyle than many others her age. And she guessed that Dylan wasn't much older than she was.

"Oh, yeah. A friend recommended it to me. Actually, she says that she met you when she was here—at a meet-up of some kind. Nina? She would have been here about three months ago, I think."

"Oh yes. Is she a photographer?"

"Yep, that's right."

Dylan laughed. "Well, I hope that she didn't have any stories to tell about me. Some of those parties can get a bit wild."

"Is that right? I guess she left that for you to tell me about."

"Oh, you think so, huh?" Dylan winked. "Not really. I'm pretty tame when it comes to partying, actually."

Isabella felt her face grow warm as it suddenly struck her that their conversation so far was feeling slightly flirtatious. She turned toward him. "Shall we go? I've been looking forward to your tour."

"Sure."

They stepped outside into the apartment parking lot and Dylan made his way to one of the motorbikes parked off to the side. Isabella followed behind, feeling slightly nervous as she realized where they were headed.

"I thought we could go on my motorbike... I have an extra helmet for you and it's just an easy way to get around."

Isabella wasn't exactly opposed to riding on the back of a motorbike in general, but somehow the idea of sitting so close to Dylan—to a perfect stranger, really—with her arms around his waist, seemed more intimate than what she was feeling comfortable with.

Dylan was waiting for her to speak and she was sure that he could tell by the reaction on her face that she wasn't as into the idea of riding on the back of the bike.

"Or we don't have to take the bike—if you're not comfortable with it." He laughed. "Which by your expression, I'm guessing you're not."

"Oh, I'm sorry. I'm sure I would get used to the idea but I think just starting out, I'd rather not. But I'm happy to pay for a taxi, or to walk—or whatever else you think would get us around to the things you want to show me."

"No worries. I'll just leave the bike here. We can walk, but let's start with a ride in a tuk-tuk. Have you been in one before?"

"Is it the little motorcycle thingy with the seat on the back? I saw them when I was out last night. That looks good to me. And no, this would be my first time in one."

"Great. I'm going to have him take us on a little driving tour around the moat that goes around the old city. It's not far at all— nothing is, really, but I think you'll find that the heat is what will get to you while walking. It takes a bit to get used to for sure."

"That sounds great. Ooh I'm excited to take my first tuk-tuk ride."

Dylan hailed a driver and negotiated a rate, a process that Isabella found entirely interesting. Nina had warned her that she should negotiate with drivers and anyone at the markets. She'd said that it was a way of life and that they enjoyed the bargaining game.

For the next thirty minutes or so, Isabella watched from the open tuk-tuk as Dylan pointed things out to her and instructed the driver where to go. She found it fascinating that one part of the city—the old town or inner city within the moat—could be so different from where she was staying.

Dylan told her that the area where they were staying—called Nimman—was the newer, more trendy area of Chiang Mai. It was where many of the digital nomads—a term Isabella instantly loved —liked to hang out because of the many cafes and co-working spaces located there.

They pulled off to the side of the road, and Isabella could see a massive temple-like structure over a wall. Dylan asked the driver to wait for them and offered her his hand so that he could help her out onto the sidewalk.

"I want to show you one of the temples. In Thailand, they're called wats, and you probably know that many Thais practice Buddhism. Chiang Mai is known for having some of the most beautiful wats and also for having so many. You'll see them all over if you're walking around the old city."

"Wow, it's so beautiful." Isabella looked up at the golden structure in front of her. There were white stone carving of elephants on either side of the entrance and within the temple there was red carpeting and what looked like an altar of sorts. "And they don't mind if we go inside?"

"No. We can go. Well, one should be dressed appropriately, which we are. No shorts or sleeveless tops. And we'll take our shoes off just over there. When you sit inside or wherever you are really, it's important to note the positioning of your feet. For Thais, the head is the most sacred part of the body and the feet are the least sacred. So, you should always take care when sitting not to point them at anyone—to sit with them tucked under you. I'll show you. Come on."

Isabella followed Dylan to where they took off their shoes and then entered into the temple to sit up front before the Buddha statue. Almost instantly, she felt at home in the quiet environment. There were a few other Thais there praying and paying their respects and she could see some monks in another area just beyond the main temple.

After several minutes, Dylan motioned to her and they got up to go back outside.

"That was great. Thanks for taking me here."

"Sure. And there are a few places that do monk chats throughout the month also. You can come and ask questions about the religion, or anything, really. It can be quite interesting, if you like that sort of thing. And there are also meditation retreats offered at a few temples nearby—one of which is at the wat on Doi Suthep. I've never done it myself, but friends of mine swear by it's being one of the most enlightening experiences they've ever had. Personally, I've not wanted to go without my computer for more than a few days." Dylan laughed.

"Hey, that reminds me—speaking of your computer—I see on your card that you're a writer?"

"I am, yes. And you? Are you on vacation?"

"Would you believe that I'm a writer too?"

"Are you?" Dylan grinned at Isabella as he helped her back into the tuk-tuk. "How 'bout we go have some lunch? I want to find out more about this beautiful new writer friend of mine."

Isabella felt herself blush as she nodded. "Lunch sounds fantastic. I'm starving. And I want to find out more about you too."

THIRTEEN

Isabella took a huge bite of her salad, taking in all the people sitting outside on the patio. Many were foreigners in small groups or solo with a laptop or book, but there were also a lot of local Thai people lunching there as well. Isabella instantly loved the place and knew that it would become one of her favorite go-to spots.

"I know it might seem lame that I brought you here instead of some cool Thai restaurant, but I figure this is a good spot to know about. You can eat a lot of delicious Thai food, but I don't know any foreigners that don't also want something else once in awhile. I'd say the local favorite salad spot is a good place to start."

"Indeed. This is perfect. Thank you for showing it to me—and for this morning. I really enjoyed the tour and the visit to the temple."

Dylan looked across the table at her and smiled. "You're welcome. It was completely my pleasure. It's always fun showing someone around here for the first time. By the way, I don't think I've asked you how long you're here for."

"Well, that's to be determined, I guess. Right now I came in without a visa, so I've only booked my apartment for a month.

They've already let me know that I can have it longer if I like, though. I suppose you're a good person to ask about all the visa stuff?"

"Oh, yes. I can tell you exactly where to go—to get the visa, but also to enjoy some neighboring countries while doing so." He caught her eye and moved his hand as if he were about to reach out and touch hers.

Isabella pulled her hand from the table into her lap, feeling awkward and unsure of what to say next.

"So, tell me about your books, Bella. What do you write?"

"I write women's fiction. Well, I've only actually published one book so far, but I'm working on a series. And also I'm only just self-published. I don't have an agent or anything cool like that."

"Hey, I don't have an agent either. I've been doing everything myself for the past five years and have learned a lot in doing so. If you need any tips or there's anything I can help you with, just ask, okay?"

"Wow. That's awesome. And your books are doing really well." Isabella caught his eye and she felt herself blush for what seemed like the hundredth time that day. "I confess. I looked you up online."

Dylan laughed. "I tried to look you up too, as a matter of fact."

"Nothing there, huh?" Isabella laughed. "I'm still early in my career. Heck, I'm not even sure if I'm any good at all. But I guess I thought that I needed to at least give it a go. Not to say that I don't love writing. It's the one thing that I've loved my entire life."

"Then I'm sure you're going to do wonderfully if you keep after it."

Dylan was quiet as he seemed to be studying her.

"What?" Isabella moved her hand toward her mouth. "Is there something on my face?"

"You're really beautiful, Bella."

I should tell him about Thomas. Isabella's heart pounded at the way Dylan was looking at her, but she didn't volunteer the information. Why wasn't she telling him?

Now she really was blushing as she thought about how to smoothly respond to Dylan's compliment. She looked over at him, noticing that he seemed slightly amused at her discomfort.

"Thank you, and you're being silly. Will we go somewhere after lunch? I don't want to keep you from something."

"You're not keeping me from anything. I thought maybe I could show you some of my favorite spots to work—just nearby and around the neighborhood. Maybe we can grab a coffee. Does that sound good? And are you feeling tired at all? That jet lag can be a real drag coming this way."

"I am getting a little tired, but your plan sounds like a good one."

"Shall we head out then?"

"We shall."

Dylan paid the bill—despite Isabella's insistence that she pay half—and they began walking down the street past where Isabella had walked the night before.

"I liked our visit to old town today, but I have to say that I'm glad I chose to live over in this neighborhood."

"Yes, I'm glad you're over on this side of town too."

Was it Isabella's imagination or did his hand just brush against hers as they walked? She stepped a bit to the right to create a little more space in between them.

They walked for a while, Isabella taking in all the shops and people that they passed. Dylan pointed out several cafes down the different streets and then they turned onto soi 12.

"Oh, I think this is the street where my friend told me to get a massage."

"Fai?"

Isabella laughed. "Wow, this place does have a small-town feel. Don't tell me that Fai is your massage person too?"

"She is, yes. And very well known among the expat community. She definitely has the magic touch. But it's more than that too. Fai is a real sweetheart. If you believe that people have callings in their lives, hers is to be a healer, that's for sure. We're going to walk right past there, so we can stop in if you'd like to book an appointment. She often books up pretty fast on the weekends, I think."

"Sure. That would be great, thanks."

Fai was busy with a client in the back, but another person took Isabella's name and booked her for an appointment in just two days. Isabella was excited that she'd been able to get in so fast.

They walked a block further, then came to the cafe that Dylan had chosen for the afternoon treat.

"I think you're going to like this place. The barista here is a master artist. You know how they make designs in the foam of the coffee drinks?"

Isabella nodded.

"Well, on the weekends here, he does portraits of people in their coffees. It's very special and fun to watch. I have a lot of friends who like to come here. The coffee is superb, the owners are great, and the wi-fi is strong."

"And also it's very cute," Isabella said as they stepped inside the door.

Dylan laughed. "Yes, it is also very cute." He waved to a small group of people sitting back in the corner with their laptops and notebooks spread out on a large table. "Great, some of my friends are here. Come on, I'll introduce you."

Isabella followed Dylan back toward the group, smiling and thinking how easy it seemed to make friends around there. Nina had been right when she'd told her about the specialness of the community and how easy it felt to stay and work from there for awhile. Isabella could already tell that it was the case, and she'd only been there not even two full days yet.

"Hi, guys. I want you to meet my new friend Bella, who just arrived in town yesterday."

Dylan went around the table and Isabella tried to do a good job of connecting names with faces so that she'd remember if she saw them around town later.

"I'll go order us some coffees. Cappuccino good for you?"

"Oh yeah, that's great, but why don't you let me get this? Please, Dylan."

"No, no. That's not necessary. You have a seat and let this crew talk your ear off trying to get to know you before I come back. Oh, and don't believe a word they say about me either."

Isabella laughed. "Noted."

They spent the next hour in the cafe, with Isabella's entire world shifting as she realized how many people were traveling or living abroad, while supporting themselves by writing or doing any number of different businesses online. She found each person that she met that day completely interesting, and it reminded her of just how fascinated she'd been when Nina had told her that she'd been making a living with her photography and her blog.

"Dylan, did you tell Bella about the party tomorrow night?" one of the guys yelled across the table.

Dylan smiled. "No, I hadn't gotten around to it yet, but since you've brought it up..." He turned toward Isabella. "A few of us— this bunch and a few more—have rented out a restaurant for the evening. There will be a local band, good food and some drinks— all the makings of what has the potential to be a fun night. I'd be happy to come pick you up, if you'd like to join us. And you can tell me tomorrow if you'd rather. No pressure."

Isabella smiled, delighted with the invitation, especially since she'd just met so many of Dylan's interesting friends. "Sure. I'd love to go. And I'm afraid I am starting to feel a bit tired. I think I should head back."

"I'll walk with you."

"Oh, you don't have to go on my account."

"No. I have to get my bike anyway. And besides, I can hang out with this lot any old time." He laughed, as did the friends that were sitting near enough to hear him.

They said their goodbyes and left the cafe, Isabella feeling more content than she'd felt in a long time—a fact that both surprised her and worried her just a bit, for reasons she couldn't quite pinpoint in the moment.

FOURTEEN

Isabella and Dylan walked along in comfortable silence. She felt surprisingly comfortable with her new friend, considering that they'd really only known one another for a day. The conversations that they'd had throughout the day, and what Dylan had shared with her about everything he'd learned while living in Thailand, had confirmed with her that her first impression of him at the airport had been correct. He really was one of the good guys—someone she could trust in her new home away from home.

The sudden thought shocked her a little. Could Chiang Mai end up becoming a home for her too, just as it had for Dylan and so many of his nomadic friends? It was different for Isabella, though. She had Thomas back home. She couldn't imagine liking a place so much that she'd ever want to be away from him for anything other than a very temporary time period.

"What are you thinking about, Bella?"

Isabella nearly jumped at the sound of Dylan's voice—she'd been so caught up in her thoughts.

"Whoa. Sorry. I guess you really were somewhere else just then. I didn't mean to startle you—or to pry." He smiled at her.

"Oh, I'm sorry. Yeah, I guess I'm just feeling a little out of it.

Must be having some jet lag after all. I'm sure a short nap will help."

"For sure. It's good to kind of ease into the time change here. Well, some people would argue differently, but I always give myself a good week before I'm back to my normal writing schedule. I'm sure you'll figure out what works for you too."

Isabella nodded and they were silent for a few minutes more.

"I really enjoyed meeting your friends today. They seem like a great group of people, all of whom were super interesting to me. I feel like I could learn a lot about my own business goals, just hanging around a crowd like that. It's quite energizing, isn't it?"

"It is for sure. It's one reason that I stay here. You can't beat the built-in community and I find everything here seems to lend itself to inspiration for me. I bet you'll find that too."

"I hope so. I think I could use some inspiration when it comes to getting back to my writing. I've really slacked off this past month or so."

"Oh, and my friends really liked you too, by the way. I could tell."

They'd reached Isabella's apartment building and she followed him over to where his motorbike was parked.

"Dylan, I can't thank you enough for showing me around today—for taking time out of your schedule to spend it with me. The entire day was perfect, and I'm so glad that I ran into you at the airport yesterday. I'd say that you've earned your stripes as best Chiang Mai tour guide to newcomers." Isabella laughed and when Dylan reached out to take her hand, she was so shocked by his touch that she just stood there, an awkward—but, if she was being honest with herself, an as-equally-excited—feeling overwhelming her.

"You don't need to thank me. I've thoroughly enjoyed spending the day with you. You're entirely pleasant to be around and I'd love the chance to get to know you better." He leaned back a little, his face relaxed and his smile confident as he looked her in the eye and leaned forward to give her a kiss.

Isabella instinctively turned her face and backed away a little so that his lips barely grazed her cheek. Her heart pounding, she pulled her hand out of his and took yet another step back. "I'm sorry. Dylan, I—"

"No, I'm sorry. I shouldn't have been so bold. Please forgive me, Bella. It's just that you looked so beautiful standing there—you've looked so beautiful all day really—and all day I've been thinking of kissing you."

Isabella's heart was still pounding fast. She didn't know quite how to react, but she did admire the way that Dylan was handling her rejection to his attempt to kiss her. He was apologetic but not embarrassed. Something about his confidence was certainly attractive.

"I—I'm sorry. I'm not quite sure what to say, really." *Tell him about Thomas! Now is definitely the time to tell him.* But she wasn't going to tell Dylan about Thomas—not yet, anyway. For some reason, she just couldn't bring herself to do it, and as he stood there still smiling at her, she felt a rush of guilt and panic all at once. What was wrong with her?

"Really, don't worry. It's too soon and you hardly know me. It was a mistake, and please don't feel awkward about it. I hope that we can just continue on, getting to know one another. I hope I've not spoiled that by trying to rush anything."

Isabella's heart had finally slowed to a normal level and she was feeling slightly more relaxed, if not a bit amused at the expression on Dylan's face now. "What? You look like you have something else that you want to say—and no, you've not spoiled anything. Of course, I still want to get to know you—as friends, I mean." *There, that was something honest.* But Isabella knew it was a cop-out.

"Well, I was just going to say—in my defense—that it's something I've learned while being here, something I've learned about myself, I mean—to seize the moment, so to speak. And that moment back then had me wanting to feel your lips on mine. I dunno, I guess it's possible that it could be just me, but I thought I was feeling some mutual attraction vibes."

He winked at her and she knew that he was teasing her just a bit.

She liked it. She liked how he flirted with her. It hit her like a huge toppling wave moving over her body. She needed to get inside her apartment to clear her head.

Dylan moved to retrieve his helmet from the locked storage of his motorbike and Isabella was grateful that his movement signified the end to what had become an awkward conversation for her. She took a deep breath in while she waited for him as he got himself organized for his ride home.

"So, are we good? Can I still pick you up for the party tomorrow? At seven o'clock? Please tell me that I've not ruined everything." He laughed and Isabella felt her body relax a bit.

Before she could even think about it, she took a few steps toward him and leaned in to give him a quick kiss on the cheek. "We're cool. And yes, seven sounds perfect. I'll see you then."

"I'll watch you until you get in the lobby." He grinned at her. "Go on."

Isabella took the few steps across the parking lot, opened the door, and turned around just as she was stepping inside.

"See you, lovely Bella. Sweet dreams."

She waved to Dylan, then turned around to make her way into the open elevator.

As soon as the doors closed, she burst into tears.

FIFTEEN

Isabella sat on the sofa taking deep breaths as she tried to get control over her tears. The day had been both wonderful and terribly confusing for her. She had no idea why she hadn't yet told Dylan about Thomas, and she knew that this was what was bothering her the most.

She reached for her phone to check her messages, cringing when she realized that she'd missed one from Thomas that he'd sent hours ago.

Hi, Babe. Just getting in and wiped out but hoping you are around to chat.

Isabella couldn't believe that she'd missed him. She felt like crying all over again as she realized that it was now six o'clock in the morning his time. Thomas was sure to be sleeping but would it be so terrible if she woke him up? It *was* Saturday.

She opened her video app, brought up his profile, and punched the send button before she could second-guess herself. Only then did she stop to think that she probably should have splashed some water on her face or at least taken the time to check that her mascara wasn't smudged under her eyes. She let the app attempt connecting several times before she gave up. Where was he?

She felt a moment of panic, but then talked herself right out of it. Of course he was sleeping at six o'clock on a Saturday morning —probably with the volume off on his phone, but quite possibly he just didn't hear it. She knew how soundly he slept, especially when he was very tired.

She sighed and pulled up his text to reply to it.

So sorry I missed you. Tried to call, but I'm sure you are sleeping. Please let's connect soon. I love you. xo

Isabella looked at the time again and then checked her world clock app. She'd send a note to Jemma to see if she'd be able to talk in the next hour or so. It was almost five o'clock in the morning in Guatemala, and Isabella knew her friend to be an early riser. It had been awhile since they'd talked on video and Isabella could really use a chat with her best friend.

She sent off the e-mail and then decided to take a quick shower. She wanted to try to stay awake until a normal bedtime, despite how tired she was suddenly feeling.

Isabella heard her phone just as she was stepping out of the shower. She threw on the robe that was hanging on the bathroom wall and grabbed her towel to dry her face as she hurried out to the living room to scoop up her phone.

Jemma.

She grinned as she clicked on the button to begin the video chat. "Jem!"

"Hey, Bella. I just got your e-mail." She laughed and Isabella saw her glance behind her to where Isabella guessed that Rafael must be sitting. "Are you decent?"

Isabella laughed too. "Yeah, sorry. I just got out of the shower, but all good. Hey, Raf."

Jemma moved her screen so that Isabella could see Rafael in

the monitor. He looked up from where he was sitting at the table drinking his coffee. "Hi, Bella, how's it going?"

"Oh, pretty good, thanks. You two are up early around there."

Jemma's face showed back on her screen. "Oh, yeah. You know me, and Raf heads to his shop around eight, so we like to have a few hours in the morning together before the day gets crazy."

"I won't keep you too long." Isabella winked.

"Oh, don't be silly. I've been dying to talk to you. I'm going to move into the bedroom actually—so Rafael can enjoy his coffee in peace."

Isabella waited until she heard a door close and Jemma's face appeared once again in the screen.

"So, tell me everything. How are you liking Thailand? Are you happy to be there?"

"Oh, yes. So far I'm loving Chiang Mai. It's so different here than Europe, Jem. I think you'd really like it. Oh, I wish you could come visit for a while. How's everything there? How's everything with you and Rafael?"

Jemma and Rafael had officially been together since he'd surprised her in coming to Tuscany with Douglas over last Christmas. For about nine months now they'd been a couple, and so far Isabella had only heard the best things about her friend's time living in Guatemala.

Jemma laughed as Isabella fired off her questions. "Oh, everything is wonderful here. Rafael is still the greatest, busy as ever with the business, though, so we don't have tons of time together other than the occasional Sunday when he doesn't go into work. But that's fine. I've met some people here—other artists mainly, which has been really cool. I'm so glad to hear that you're liking it there. You know I can't wait to see you, but I think it's going to be a while. Well, you are always welcome to come here. You know that. I'm planning to head to the orphanage for a few weeks while Tori goes to the States to take care of some things. Bella, you really should come to the orphanage sometime." Jemma stopped talking for a moment and then laughed. "Wow. Sorry for talking your ear off there. Now, it's your turn. Tell me all about Thailand, and how are things with you and Thomas since you've left?"

Isabella felt a knot in her stomach at the mention of Thomas's name. How much should she tell Jemma?

"Bella? I can see your face, you know." Jemma laughed. "What's going on? Are you okay?"

"Yeah, I'm okay. Well, something kinda weird just happened. But in general, things are fine."

"Well, you can talk to me about anything. You know that, right?"

Isabella felt some relief as she went on to talk then to her best friend about so many things that had been on her mind lately—the weirdness she'd been feeling in New York, her first impressions of Thailand, and finally, the odd situation that she'd just found herself in with Dylan. She stopped talking and grabbed a tissue from her purse to dab at her eyes while she waited for Jemma's assessment of everything.

"So what exactly has you so upset? Is it that your feelings for Thomas are changing?"

"No. Not at all. I love Thomas, Jemma. I don't want anything to change between us, but—"

"But?"

"Oh, I don't know. I guess I'm afraid that things will change— that he'll make a different decision about me while I'm gone. If I'm being honest, I'm shocked that I did leave, now that I'm sitting here expressing this all to you."

"Well, it seems to me like you made a good decision for yourself. Not that it's about being away from him, but you and I both know that it's hard to make things work if your heart is somewhere else. And it seems to me that your heart—your gut, or whatever you want to call it—was telling you that your time for traveling wasn't over. I don't think that can be a bad thing, Bella. We're so young, right?"

"I know. You're right. Do you feel settled? There with Rafael, I mean? Are you content with your decision to move there with him, Jem?"

Jemma took her time to answer as she seemed to be thinking about the question. "I am content, I'd say. But it's not like I don't also think about traveling again, especially when I'm hearing about your adventures." She laughed. "But I've done more travel than you have, also—with my mom and Chase when I was younger—so maybe it's not as big of a deal for me at this point, you know."

"Yeah, that makes sense."

"But Bella—I think the bigger question is how you're feeling about this guy? Dylan, is it? You know I love Thomas and the thought of you two being together, but you're young—we're young. No one would fault you for not wanting to be serious with one person at this point in your life. I know, I'd never hold that against you. Do you feel like that's something you need to maybe think about?"

Isabella sighed. She knew the answer before Jemma had even asked the question. Thomas was everything to her, the man she was meant to be with. Any feelings that she might be having about anyone else would only ever pale in comparison to the man she'd known for almost her entire life.

"No, I think it's easy to get caught up in the moment—that it would be with Dylan—just because he seems to have a way of making me feel so wanted or something. And I guess it's just kinda weird being here, so far away from Thomas. In the back of my head, there's a little voice telling me that he's going to meet someone else, that things are going to change between us and that I might need to prepare myself for that. But that's not anything I'd ever want to happen."

"Well, then it seems to me that you just need to clue Dylan in on the fact that you have a boyfriend—you know, like you said." Jemma smiled at her. "You know what you're doing, Bella. Use this time for yourself. I think if you do that, you can't go wrong, and I have the feeling that it will only make your relationship with Thomas that much stronger, actually."

"Really? You think so?"

Jemma nodded. "I do. You second-guess yourself too much sometimes, you know."

"Yes, and you know me so well. How am I ever living without you in my life every day?" Isabella laughed in the camera at her friend's silly expression.

"I don't know. I guess you need to come down here for a long visit. Seriously, we need to make that happen. Maybe you and Thomas should come during his spring break this year. Raf and I would love that."

"We'll see. It sounds like if I stay here for a while, he'd be coming over this way to see me—that we'd do some exploring together in this part of the world while I'm here. But I do agree that we should come there very soon. It would be a fun reunion." Isabella tried and failed to stifle a yawn.

"On that note, it looks like someone could use a good sleep. I'm so glad that we were finally able to connect. I miss you, girl." Jemma blew a kiss toward Isabella on the screen.

She laughed. "Oh, I miss you too. Thanks for listening, Jem. You're the best. Really. Have a good day."

Isabella hung up feeling much better and more resolved than ever. Nothing bad had happened. So far, she was loving her new home and she'd made a great new friend. She went to bed feeling confident that she only needed to be honest with Dylan—that it would alleviate any weird feelings she was having and everything would be fine afterward.

And talk to Thomas. She really needed to connect with Thomas soon.

SIXTEEN

Isabella laughed at Dylan as he stood in front of her holding out the helmet. In not getting on the bike with him, was she making a bigger deal of things than what was necessary? She could be near him just fine. Nothing was going to happen, because they were only going to be friends.

"Bella, I wanna take you for a ride." He grinned at her. "The party's not that far away and also—just so you know—I have no intention of drinking tonight. You have my word that it's always safety first with me, but especially if I'm entrusted with lovely you on the back of my bike."

Isabella returned the smile, thinking that she rather enjoyed his persistence and also feeling like maybe she had something to prove —to herself anyway. She nodded. "Okay, you're on. But only because I'm not the kinda girl who's bothered with having helmet hair."

They laughed together and Isabella pulled on her helmet as she followed Dylan to where he'd parked the motorbike. He turned around to help her with the strap that she'd been having trouble with and her heart jumped a little at the light feel of his fingers so close to her face. *Stop it, Iz.* She tried to inhale a deep breath without his noticing while he turned on the bike and backed it out of its spot.

"Climb on."

Isabella obeyed, taking care to situate the long skirt that she wore so that most of it was tucked well underneath her. "Okay, ready when you are, I guess."

"I think you better hold on." Dylan laughed. "I don't wanna lose you while rounding our first corner."

"Oh, right." Isabella moved her hands awkwardly around to the side, looking for something to hold onto besides Dylan.

"Bella, I don't bite you, know." He turned his head enough so that she could see him wink at her. "So, feel free to put your arms around my waist or if you're not comfortable with that, there's a bar just behind where you're sitting. Grab that with one or both hands and you should be just fine. Or, as I said, just hold on to me."

Isabella laughed, appreciating the fact that things seemed fine between them, despite the awkward moment from the day before. They'd talked on the phone earlier that day when Dylan had called to apologize again, which had helped to solidify to Isabella that everything was going to be okay.

She reached around to grab onto the bar as Dylan had suggested and once they started moving out of the parking lot, she rested her other hand lightly on his back.

She'd slept in that morning and then gone for a big walk around the neighborhood. She'd taken it easy all afternoon, catching up on e-mails and working out some plot points for the current book she was working on. By the time Dylan had arrived to pick her up, she'd had a restful day and felt that the party was going to be the perfect way to end it.

Now she was happy that she'd agreed to go on the bike with him. She loved the feel of the slight breeze hitting her face and the easy way they were able to move through traffic. Dylan seemed more than capable as a driver and she instantly felt safe behind him.

He turned as they waited at a traffic light. "How are you doing back there? Everything okay?"

"Yes, I love it!"

"Great—I'd like to take you for a proper ride one of these days, if you're up for it. There's a lot to see just driving out in the countryside a bit. I think you'd really enjoy it."

The light changed and they were moving again before Isabella had a chance to respond. Within minutes, Dylan had turned unto a busy street and into the parking lot of what seemed to be quite the happening restaurant. He parked the motorbike and waited for her to get off from behind him.

"There, now that wasn't so bad, was it?" he teased her as she handed him her helmet and brushed her fingers through her hair before pulling it up into a loose bun on top of her head.

"No, I quite liked it, actually. And this place looks great, by the way." She had glanced past him to see the outdoor seating in a garden, complete with a small pond and strands of twinkling lights up in the trees above them.

"Yeah, it's one of our favorites around here—our go-to spot for parties and anything bigger than a small get-together." He held his arm out for her to take his elbow. "Come on, you'll love the food. There's a buffet set up inside and everything is delicious."

Isabella linked her arm through his, letting him lead her inside to the buffet table.

"Are you hungry? Shall we get our plates?"

"Yes, I am. That sounds great."

They piled their plates high with many Thai dishes that Isabella had yet to try, and as they were making their way outside, Isabella heard someone calling out to them from a large corner table."

"Dylan, Bella—come join us."

Isabella smiled as she recognized the people that she'd met the other day plus many more new faces who were quickly introduced to her when they sat down.

Dylan stood behind her. "Let me go get our drinks. What would you like?"

"I'll have a wine please—red. Thank you." Isabella didn't really drink much alcohol, but occasionally she did like to have some wine with her dinner and tonight felt like such an occasion to her.

She settled into her chair and turned toward the woman to her right, who was speaking to her.

"Hi, Bella. I'm sure you've already forgotten most of our names. I'm—"

"Wait, don't tell me. Ann, right?"

"Hey, I'm impressed." Ann smiled widely at her. "I'm so glad that you could join us tonight."

"Thanks for inviting me. It's nice to feel so welcomed. I really appreciate it. How long have you been here?"

"I've been in Chiang Mai for almost five months now, but before this I was living down south on the islands—well, mostly Koh Samui—for about a year."

"Wow!"

Ann laughed. "Yeah, it's safe to say that Thailand can really grow on you. For some people, anyway. I love everything about it. So, how are you and Dylan getting on? He's such a romantic, that one."

"Oh no. I mean, Dylan and I are just friends." Isabella felt the telltale sign of heat rising to her cheeks.

"Really? I'm guessing that you might need to tell him that." Ann motioned her head toward where Dylan was standing by the bar. "The way he looks at you...I'd say he's pretty smitten. He's a good guy, Bella. One could definitely do a lot worse."

"Yes, he is a good guy." Isabella took a bite of her food, desperate to change the topic of conversation and grateful when Dylan arrived back with her drink moments later.

"Were your ears burning just now? Because I was really talking you up to Bella here," Ann said as Dylan sat down on the other side of Isabella.

"Oh, were you now?" Dylan grinned and held his glass of soda up in the air slightly. "A toast, if I may…"

Isabella and Ann raised their glasses in front of them.

"To friendships—both old and new."

The three clinked glasses and Ann got up from the table.

"I'll talk to you both later. Good to see you again, Bella."

"You too."

Dylan turned his attention toward her. "How's your food? Are you enjoying it?"

"I am, thank you. And thank you for the wine too, by the way."

"It's my pleasure."

As the night progressed, Isabella thoroughly enjoyed the conversation—with Dylan and several others who were seated at their table. When the band started to play, they danced to a few of the faster songs and Isabella had one more glass of wine. She was feeling completely relaxed and unaware of just how tired she was until Dylan commented on her yawning.

He laughed when she told him that she wasn't quite ready to leave. "I think we should get you home, party girl. Shall we?"

Isabella tried to hide another yawn behind her hand, but gave up laughing with him. "Yeah, I suppose so." She followed him out toward the parking lot and when he took her hand, she didn't resist. She felt safe with Dylan, and for some reason that seemed incredibly important to her all of a sudden. It probably had something to do with the fact that it had been ages since she'd had wine to drink. That, along with her sleepiness, had her feeling slightly unsteady on her feet.

Dylan smiled at her as he reached over to gently release her hair from her elastic band and tuck it behind her ears as he'd probably seen her do earlier. He put her helmet on, strapping it under her chin, then put his own on and backed the bike out of the space.

"Climb on, pretty lady."

She tossed one leg over and then the other, and then did the best she could to be sure that her skirt was not going to fly up to the point of revealing her unmentionables.

Dylan laughed as he reached back to help her tuck it a little tighter underneath her. He then reached directly behind him, taking both of her hands in his as he placed them firmly around his waist. "I think you better hold on to me now." He laughed, and again Isabella didn't argue with him.

As he pulled onto the road and the breeze struck her face, she held onto him just a bit tighter, resting her face against his back. She breathed in deeply, noticing that his cologne was one of her favorite scents.

In what felt like no time at all, they were pulling into the parking lot of her apartment building. Dylan again took her hands, giving them a quick squeeze before she climbed off the bike, feeling just slightly wobbly when her feet touched the ground. He removed first his helmet and then her own and before she even knew what was happening he was kissing her.

And she was kissing him back.

His hands reached up into her hair, pulling her face closer to his when they stopped momentarily to look at one another. They broke for only a second before their lips were locked again.

What am I doing? Stop it, Isabella. And just like that her mind became crystal clear as she pushed him slightly away from her, breaking their embrace. "Dylan, stop. I'm so sorry. I shouldn't—I shouldn't be doing this."

He reached out to take her hand, but this time she pulled hers away just as fast.

"Bella, what's wrong? I know you feel something too. We don't have to do more than kiss. I promise you that I'm a gentleman." He smiled and leaned forward, trying to kiss her again.

"No, Dylan. I should have told you—I'm sorry. I have a

boyfriend. I can't do this. I thought we could be friends but—but this isn't going to work. I'm sorry. I have to go."

She heard him calling out to her as she ran toward the door, but her own frantic thoughts drowned his words out. All she wanted was to be alone in her apartment to make sense of what had just happened.

Her thoughts turned toward Thomas as she felt the first pang of regret.

What had she just done?

SEVENTEEN

Isabella heard her phone ringing just as she was entering her apartment. Even though she assumed it would be Dylan calling her, she pulled her phone out to see that it was actually her video app sounding with an incoming call.

It was Thomas.

She didn't even give herself a moment to think about how she looked. Almost certainly there were signs of tears on her face but she was desperate to speak to him. She walked to the kitchen to get a glass of water while she waited the few seconds for their call to connect.

"Iz, are you there?"

There he was. Isabella smiled and felt her earlier panicked feelings vanish. She just needed to connect with Thomas and everything would feel better. She hadn't done anything wrong. Not really—nothing she couldn't move on from anyway.

"Thomas! I miss you so much." She grinned into the phone as she lay down on the sofa.

"I miss you too, babe. Sorry it's been so hard to connect. Iz, are you okay?"

Isabella's fingers went to her face as she now noticed the mascara under her eyes on the screen in front of her.

"You look like you've been crying."

He frowned into the screen at her and it was all she could do to keep from bursting into tears right then. She so desperately wanted to be curled up on Thomas's sofa in his arms right that moment—not halfway across the world.

"Iz?"

"Oh, I just miss you." She smiled, hoping that he'd be satisfied with her answer.

"Well, you look kinda dressed up and it is after 1:00 a.m. there. Have you been meeting some fun people? Tell me everything."

"Yes, I've just come from a party, actually." She could tell him everything—just leave out the part about her new friend Dylan kissing her—or more importantly, the fact that she'd kissed him back. She tried to push the scene out of her head as she told Thomas everything she'd been dying to tell him since she'd arrived.

He listened intently, laughing as she shared some of her moments of confusion with her attempt to speak Thai and various other humorous things that can only occur when one is in a different country—the kinds of things that inspired her to travel and learn about other cultures—and also the very types of things that she'd experienced with Thomas during their earlier travel together.

She heard Thomas's phone ding with an incoming text and waited as he checked it.

"Everything okay?"

"Yeah. I don't want to—not at all—but I'm going to have to go in a few minutes."

"Really? We've barely had any time." Isabella tried not to sound too disappointed, but it felt important to her that their time was getting cut short.

"Sorry, Iz. I've got study group in an hour."

"Well, tell me about school quick. I've been doing all the talking and you've barely said two words."

She thought she saw something flash across his face before he answered her. What was it? *Don't be paranoid, Isabella.*

"Oh, school's fine. You know—school is school. Exhausting, slightly frustrating and well, what else is there to say, really?"

"Well, that doesn't sound very positive. Are you happy with your classes?"

"Happy enough. Oh, I don't know. Maybe we can talk about it later. Right now, I'm starting to freak out about my biology exam on Monday." He laughed. "And by the way, please remind me why we decided that I need to have Biology when you helped me pick out my classes for the semester?"

Isabella laughed too. Thomas had always disliked his science classes—even back in middle school when they'd dissected their first frog together.

"Because it's one of your prerequisites—you know, in case you want to graduate or something."

Thomas laughed. "Right. I remember now. Well, it's driving me a bit bonkers and I can't for the life of me think of what good it's going to do for me with my business degree. And remind me why I decided I needed to get this degree at all?"

"Thomas." Isabella was surprised at how he seemed to be feeling about school, but she didn't want to say anything that wasn't supportive. Maybe he was just tired. He looked tired to her.

"Yes? I'm waiting." He winked at her.

"Well, you tell me why you want the degree. I know you want to do something with business but if you want to follow in your father's footsteps, I think there are other ways you can learn. To be honest, ever since I've known you, I always thought you'd end up just doing your own entrepreneurial thing after high school. You were always the kid who could convince anyone to buy anything from you."

"So you're saying I should become a car salesman." Thomas

laughed, and Isabella loved it that he looked slightly more relaxed now.

"No. I'm saying that you're smart and I believe that you'd be successful with or without college."

Isabella had always admired Thomas from the moment she'd met him in grade school. While other kids had been out playing and getting into mischief on the weekends, he'd been busy setting up his lemonade stand or wheeling and dealing down at the local pawn shop with various collector's items that he'd purchased online. Thomas had always been the kind of smart that one didn't learn from books.

"Thanks for saying that, Iz." Thomas smiled at her in a way that made her heart ache to hug him. "I do miss you, babe. So much. I wish you were here right now."

Isabella felt a lump in her throat. "Me too. Are you gonna be okay?"

"Yeah. Sorry, Iz. I don't want you to worry about me. I'm sure I'm just feeling funky because of this test coming up. I guess I just need to figure out a way to manage my stress better." He grinned at her on the screen.

"What's that smile for?"

"Well, I feel like this conversation is a Freaky Friday moment or something."

"I'm not sure that I know what that means." Isabella was appreciating that his mood had gotten a lot lighter.

"You know, like we've switched places or something. Wasn't it not that long ago that I was talking you down off the ledge from being all stressed out about school or whatever else you were stressing your pretty little head out about?"

"Right. And you were the one skipping classes and acing your tests without even studying for ten minutes."

"Yep. And now you're the one skipping—around the world or whatever it is that you're doing over there."

Thomas laughed, but a vision of Dylan and her kissing only

moments before flashed through her mind, causing her to feel sick to her stomach. What was she doing over here?

"Well, I just want you to be happy, Thomas. And you know that we can do a better job—I can do a better job—figuring out this time thing so that we can talk more—if you need to, I mean. Just name the time and I'll make sure to be available, even if it's in the middle of the night."

"Thanks, honey."

Isabella thought it looked like he wanted to say something else. "What?"

"Oh, nothing. I just so wish that I could kiss you right now."

"I know. Me too." It was Thomas that she desperately wanted to kiss—*only* Thomas. "I better let you go now."

"Yeah, okay. I'm really glad that we finally talked. You get a good night's sleep and we'll talk soon."

Isabella nodded, trying not to cry because she was missing him so much.

"I love you, Iz."

"I love you too, Thomas."

She put her phone on the coffee table and rested her head back against the sofa. She was glad that she'd spoken to Thomas. It had made her feel mostly a lot better—mostly, because it also didn't help the incredible guilt she was feeling about what had just happened with Dylan.

Why had she kissed him back? Was it just the wine that had made her act so impulsively?

She knew how she felt about Thomas—that was not going to change—but for some reason, she wasn't handling Dylan's affection for her in the right way. Maybe now that he knew she had a boyfriend, he'd give up altogether on any thoughts of their being more than friends. She had no reason to think otherwise. After all, she was the one responsible for not being direct with him about her relationship in the first place.

And after talking to Thomas, she felt a new resolve about the commitment she had with him. Thomas wasn't going to leave her, and she needed to be careful not to ever give him reason to.

He didn't need to know about the kiss. It wouldn't do any good to tell him that.

But as she had the thought, her stomach ached. She'd always been honest with Thomas.

EIGHTEEN

Isabella sat in the small massage room waiting for Fai. She would have forgotten about the appointment altogether, had it not been for the reminder that she'd set on her phone. She'd woken up late and had still been feeling a bit out of sorts because of what had happened the night before with Dylan.

She was thankful for the massage appointment. Getting a Thai massage was the one thing, other than eating the great food, that everyone seemed to agree was a necessary highlight when visiting Thailand.

She heard a light knock on the door.

"Come in."

"Good morning."

The woman who entered the room was not more than five feet tall, if even that. She had a very slight frame, typical of most of the Thai women that Isabella had seen so far. She was older than Isabella had pictured for some reason. If she had to guess, she'd put her in her late fifties or early sixties, but she was reminded of a conversation that had taken place at the party the night before— about how gracefully Thai women seemed to age. Ann had laughed about it, telling Isabella not to be shocked when she met older Thai women who would gleefully share their age.

The small woman was smiling and offering her hand to Isabella. "You must be Isabella? I'm Fai. Great to meet you."

Isabella returned the smile and the firm handshake. "Yes, you can call me Bella if you like. Good to meet you, Fai. I've heard many wonderful things about you."

Fai's grin grew even wider—something that Isabella would have thought impossible as it was already the fullest smile she'd ever seen.

"Oh, really? My clients—they are so wonderful. Everybody love Fai and I love everybody.

"Now, we should get you started, yes? You want ninety minutes?" Fai reached over to touch Isabella's shoulder. "I think you need long massage. Too much stress. I can tell in your body."

Isabella laughed, feeling instantly at ease with her. "Ninety minutes it is then."

"Okay, great. You get on table."

"Okay, do I need to take off my clothes, or..."

"Do you want?"

Isabella felt confused as her question came back to her.

"Oh, Thai massage—it's okay with clothes. You put this on. Over there." She handed Isabella some clothing and pointed toward the curtain in the corner of the room.

Isabella heard the faint sounds of what sounded like a waterfall as she pulled the light fabric over her head. She unfolded the pants, staring at them for a good minute or so as she realized she had no idea how to put them on. They were of the same fabric as the top but seemed, by the size of the waist, to be made for someone much larger than herself.

"Excuse me. Fai?"

"Yes. Are you okay in there, Bella? Do you need help with the pants?"

"Yes, I think you gave me the wrong size." She peered around the edge of the curtain, holding the pants out in front of her.

Fai, laughed. "Can I help? You are not too modest?"

Isabella laughed too, opening the curtain to herself in her underwear.

Fai walked over to take the pants from her. "They are what you say in English fisherman pants. Very comfortable. Only one size. See?" She lifted her top up a bit so that Isabella could see the way the fabric folded and tied at the waist.

"Oh, cool."

Fai held the pants out so that Isabella could step into them. Then she showed her how to fold first one side and then the other so that the two sides met in the middle, causing the pants to be the proper fit. Then she folded down the waist and tied it with the attached strings.

"There you are like Thai now. You like?"

Isabella moved out of the dressing area. "Yes, they feel great, actually. I'm going to have to get me a pair of them."

"Yes, go to Saturday market. Don't pay first price. Good deal." Fai winked. "Now you get on the table. Back first. We start with feet."

Fai walked across the room to turn the lights down low as Isabella lay back on the table. Fai positioned her chair at the end of the table and soon Isabella felt the pressure of her fingers on the bottoms of her feet.

"It's okay? Good pressure?"

"Yes, it's okay."

"Good. You close eyes. Relax. I can fix a lot of your problems when I fix your feet."

Isabella smiled. If only life were that simple and Fai could fix all her problems. She closed her eyes and tried to clear her mind as Fai worked on one foot and then the other. So far, her touch *was* really good. She'd been lucky to get the recommendation.

Before long, Fai moved from Isabella's feet and legs to her

hands and arms. Isabella was shocked at how good it felt to have her hands massaged. She didn't think about it often, but when she was in a good writing groove her hands would often bother her from all the typing.

She'd do well to schedule as much regular massage as possible while it was so easily available to her. Dylan had said that it wasn't uncommon at all for people there to go for massage every other day or even daily.

"Okay. Now you turn over. Time for back and neck. This will be very good for you, Bella."

Isabella turned over and very soon after felt the pressure of Fai's knees on the back of her legs as her hands worked on Isabella's lower back. She stifled a laugh. It felt odd to her, but she'd already gotten a heads-up that Thai massage very much involved the body of the person giving the massage too.

"Ooh. Ow."

"You have big knot. Let me work on it, okay? You take deep breaths."

"Okay, but maybe a little less hard please." Isabella did trust her and she'd had massages before, so she was aware that often the healing was worth the pain in the short term.

She felt Fai's hands move to her neck. Isabella breathed in deeply and tried to focus her thoughts on the pain and stress leaving her body. As she relaxed more and more, she suddenly felt a huge emotional release, unlike anything she'd ever experienced in a similar situation.

As Fai's hands worked up and down on her shoulders and across her upper back, Isabella couldn't hold her tears back. Her instinct was to be embarrassed but just as soon as her tears were falling, Fai gently asked her to sit up while she positioned herself Indian style where Isabella's head had been.

She placed a pillow in her lap. "Okay. Lie here. Now I will massage your head. You relax. Tears are good. Means my hands are healing you." She winked at Isabella.

Isabella smiled and then lay down again with her head on the pillow. Fai was unlike anyone Isabella had ever met before. She sure did seem to have a gift. Isabella could feel it already—physically and emotionally.

Fai ran her fingers through Isabella's hair, giving little tugs when she got to the ends. Isabella had stopped crying and felt the warm cloth that Fai placed across her face, wiping her cheeks and eyes gently.

"Tears are cleansing. Do you feel better, Bella?"

"I do. Thank you. I don't even know exactly why I was crying."

Fai finished with the cloth on Isabella's face and began rubbing her temples in a circular motion. "Our bodies hold on to our sadness—and our worries, our fears...everything we don't want to talk about, you know?"

Isabella nodded slightly, enjoying the sensation of Fai's fingers pressing on her head. She could hardly believe how relaxed she was feeling.

Fai continued, her voice soothing and deliberate with her words. "I release tension in the body but also in the heart sometimes." She placed her hand gently over Isabella's heart, before moving both hands deliberately to her head. "And also in the head. Some people—they think too much. Maybe this is you, Bella?"

Isabella opened her eyes and grinned up at her. "That is entirely possible."

Fai laughed and then gently pushed her up from the pillow. "Now we are finished. I will get you some tea while you change."

"Wow, thank you so much. That felt really good."

"You are welcome. You do good job of receiving my energy too." She smiled and then walked toward the door. "I'll be right back. Go change. Then we talk."

Isabella changed back into her clothes and then Fai sat with her for a good ten minutes as she drank her tea.

"I hope I'm not keeping you from another client or anything."

"No. I always give myself half hour in between. Because sometimes I like my client. Like you. I want to sit with them awhile. Find out things. And also rest my hands." She laughed.

"That makes perfect sense to me."

"Bella, can I say something to you?"

Isabella nodded, unsure why the sudden question made her feel slightly on edge.

"You are young girl. Very pretty. And I think successful. I feel in your body—in your energy—that you must quiet your mind a little bit. Maybe you worry too much."

Isabella couldn't help the tears. It wasn't that she was feeling particularly bad. It was the way that Fai spoke to her so intently that seemed to touch her. It was as if the older woman knew something very deep and very wise about her.

Fai reached out, placing her hand gently on Isabella's knee. "Maybe you just need some time to quiet your mind. I have a place I recommend to you. For meditation. A very good place for healing retreat. People go here and they come back feeling free. I think you should be free too, Bella."

"Thank you." Isabella was both laughing and crying at the same time. She didn't quite know what to make of Fai and her impressions of her but she was very aware of taking it all in. She trusted her intentions, anyway.

Fai wrote down the name of the retreat center and Isabella booked another appointment with her. She left feeling both good and exhausted as she made her way down the street to find some lunch.

NINETEEN

Isabella looked down at her phone when she heard the ding of an incoming message. Rats. It was the first that she'd looked at her phone since before the massage and now she realized that she'd missed two calls from Dylan. She clicked on the incoming message to read his text that had just come in.

Bella, can you call me when you get a chance? I just want to make sure that everything is okay. And I think we should talk.

She bit into her bottom lip as she thought about how to reply to him. She so wanted to avoid him altogether—but that wasn't fair or likely. She was sure that they'd be running into one another around town, especially since he practically lived around the corner from her.

She took a bite of her salad and just as she was constructing a reply, she noticed Dylan sitting across the room at a table by himself. At first she was completely taken aback that they happened to be lunching at the same place at the moment of his text, but then again he had told her that it was one of his favorite spots, so she supposed it wasn't all that weird.

So, what to do? She felt incredibly awkward and mostly

wanted to quietly leave out the door in the back. But just as she was calling her waiter over to ask for the bill, Dylan caught her eye and waved slightly in her direction before he got up from where he was sitting to walk toward her.

Well, that's one way to handle things, I suppose—like a band-aid. Let's just clear the air.

"Bella, hi. Mind if I sit down for a minute?"

"No, go ahead. Sorry, I was just about to text you. I just came from my massage so I'm only now seeing your missed calls."

"No worries. I just wanted to clear the air—about last night. And make sure that there are no hard feelings between us."

Isabella really did appreciate his directness. It was refreshing the way that he didn't seem to dance around things that were on his mind. She could probably learn a thing or two from him in that regard.

"Well, I know that I don't have any bad feelings. Not toward you anyway. Possibly toward myself maybe, but that's for me to deal with, not you."

"I will say that I was feeling more than a little taken aback when you told me that you had a boyfriend. I was sure that I was getting some signals from you—maybe that's what you're feeling bad about, but you don't need to as far as I'm concerned. I only wish you would have told me earlier—about your boyfriend. I'm not one to mess around like that and I never would have pursued anything with you beyond friendship, had I known."

Isabella nodded. "You're a good guy, Dylan."

"Well, I'll leave it up to you but if you want to be friends, I'm all for it. And it won't be a problem. I can promise you that."

Isabella believed him. If things were going to be weird or awkward around Dylan, it would be because of her, not him.

"Thanks. I appreciate that. And I am really grateful for meeting you. You've helped to make the transition here for me so much easier. I actually can't believe how at home I'm feeling, which is better than I ever anticipated."

"Good, Bella. I'm glad. Now tell me, how was your massage? Did you love Fai?"

"Oh, yes I did. She's really great and I'm definitely going back regularly."

"Super. Well, I'm gonna run. A bunch of us are meeting at a cafe later this afternoon—for work. I can text you the address if you're interested in joining us."

"Sure. That would be great. Thanks."

Dylan waved and Isabella watched him walk out to his motorbike parked in front of the restaurant. He really did seem very easygoing, and she felt completely different about being around him than she had earlier that morning. What had happened last night really had been her fault for not mentioning Thomas to him. She sighed because she still didn't know what had possessed her not to share that information. But she wouldn't waste time overthinking things. If she learned anything from Fai that morning, it was that her thoughts were affecting her body and her mind, and she wanted to work on being healthier all around.

Isabella pulled out her notebook and decided to do some planning. She really needed to get a handle on the book that she'd been plotting for the past few weeks. She felt like she was in a good place to finally get it to completion while she was in Thailand. She just needed to make her writing a higher priority once again.

Her phone dinged with a message from Dylan with the address of the coffee shop. She pulled up the map on her phone to see that the cafe was only a few blocks away from her apartment. She had time to go home for a short nap and a shower. Then she'd see how she felt about going out for work.

Isabella rolled over in her bed to look at the time on her phone. Her short nap had turned into two hours, which meant that she'd forego the cafe meeting for today. She needed to break in her new workspace at the apartment anyway.

She pulled up Dylan's text to let him know that she wasn't coming and after she'd sent the message realized that she'd missed two texts from Thomas. She calculated New York time to be three o'clock in the morning. She wouldn't wake him—not this time. She smiled as she read his texts to her.

I miss you, babe. Call me when you get this? Love u. xo

And then again about thirty minutes later...

Where are you? Going to bed now. Let's talk tomorrow?

She texted him back, wanting him to see her note first thing in the morning.

So sorry I missed you. How's the studying going? Let's try for tomorrow. Love u. xo

It felt good to be communicating with Thomas regularly. It felt easier and harder at the same time. It felt like she'd been away from him for ages, when in reality it hadn't even been a week yet. Had it really only been a few days since she'd touched down in Thailand?

She jumped out of bed and into the shower. She was determined to get a few hours of some work done before dinner. It was time. She was ready to settle in and get to the business of what she'd come there for—time for herself. Fine if she made some friends and had occasional meetings in cafes, but this trip was really for learning more about herself.

She settled in at her desk and opened up her laptop. She did a quick search for the name of the retreat center that Fai had written down for her. And then she got lost in reading all about the offerings and programs. Most of them were silent retreats that included schedules and periods of meditation and fasting. She could learn more about Buddhism from monks. For all of the programs, phones and computers were highly discouraged and there wasn't easy access to wi-fi, although it did exist for emergency situations.

It was interesting to think about—living in silence without technology at her fingertips. She couldn't imagine if this would be a good thing for her or something that would drive her absolutely crazy. If she trusted Fai—and for some reason, she really did—the retreat could be exactly the thing she needed right now.

TWENTY

Isabella watched out the window as the taxi driver made his way up a fairly steep hill. The retreat center was a good hour's drive from town, and she was really enjoying the countryside. She'd booked herself in for seven nights—something she'd thought long and hard about before finally telling herself that she could always leave early if it wasn't going to be a good fit for her.

It didn't sound like it would be easy, that was for sure. But the reviews and personal recommendations that she'd gotten about the experience had been enough to convince her, especially because of where her head had been lately in regards to what had happened between her and Dylan. She still felt incredibly guilty about the whole situation and still wondered how much she should share with Thomas—or if she even should tell Thomas.

Thinking about him now reminded her about the quick call they'd had the night before. She planned to fully embrace the "no technology" suggestion while at the retreat, so having that last chat with him had been difficult. But she could contact him if she really needed to. She'd brought her phone with her just in case.

She really did have a hard time imagining how the guests were able to live in almost complete silence for such long periods of time. There would be regularly scheduled meetings with her advisor while there, and also a daily group session with the monks that involved learning about Buddhism and the benefits of meditation and fasting.

She took a deep breath of cool air through the open window of the taxi. She'd survive. And hopefully she'd come away fresh with new book ideas and a more peaceful state of mind—that was her main goal in doing the retreat, anyway.

They pulled up to the gate; it was opened by a guard of sorts. Right away Isabella was taken by the beauty of the place. The stone wall on either side of the gate had large elaborate carvings of elephants. An expansive lake with a tree-lined walkway was directly in front of them and Isabella could count three massive fountains just in her current line of vision. They passed by a big open temple to her right where she could make out a group of people sitting on the red-carpeted floor as they seemed to be listening to something going on inside.

The taxi driver drove just a little further around the lake until they came to a building with a big welcome sign out front. Isabella got her one modest bag from the trunk and paid the driver. Before she could barely turn around, a young Thai woman, dressed in beautiful traditional clothing, was by her side to take her suitcase from her.

"Hello, you are Miss Isabella?"

"Yes, that's me. Thank you."

"Welcome. I am Malee. We are so happy to have you with us. Follow me, please."

Isabella followed her to a golf cart and within minutes, Malee had her at another building about a quarter mile from the entrance.

"We have you booked into the suite. It's quite nice. You will like it."

There had been three different accommodation options to choose from—all of which included private sleeping areas—but

Isabella had opted for the deluxe accommodation that was completely private, including her own bathroom. She figured that her seven-day adventure was going to be difficult enough. If she wanted to splurge on the living arrangement while she sat in silence contemplating her life, she'd not feel bad about it.

"What's that over there?" Isabella pointed to the far side of the lake, where she had spotted another group of smaller buildings that looked like little cabins.

"Oh, those are also accommodations. Small villas that are quite nice. Not for retreat guests. Tourists and people who just want to spend some time by the lake and in nature."

Isabella nodded and made a mental note to find out more information about it. If she enjoyed her stay here, maybe it would be some place that she'd bring Thomas when he came to visit—*if* he came to visit.

Isabella shook her head as if doing so could erase the thought. *Starting now—less with the negative, more with the positive, Iz.*

She followed her hostess up the short walkway and through the door of her suite. It looked exactly as it had in the pictures—basic, in terms of the furniture, but comfortable enough, and the view of the lake was spectacular. It was one of the main reasons that she'd booked the suite. She figured that a nice view would help her when it came to quieting her mind, if that was even a genuine possibility. *Ugh, stop it with the negative again.*

She brought her attention back to Malee, who was slipping her shoes back on in the doorway.

"Oh, your room actually does have wi-fi. If you need it, the code is in the top drawer of your desk."

Rats! She could have brought her computer after all and possibly gotten a lot of writing done. She practically laughed out loud at herself for being so ridiculous. No. She was not here to work. She was here to grow, to learn about herself. There would be plenty of time for work after her retreat.

"So, if you could just come to the main hall anytime this afternoon, you can meet with your adviser and she will also take you to the restaurant for dinner. Today will be your last day of regular food before you start fasting with the others tomorrow. Light meals for breakfast and lunch. No eating past three o'clock. You can get water, juices, and teas any time you like."

"Oh, wow. I hope that I can do this."

"I think you will be surprised. It is not so difficult after the first day." She smiled. "And—well, if you get very hungry, you are always welcome to go to the restaurant. It's where the non-retreat guests eat, and the chef is really very good." She winked at Isabella and then reached out to place her hand on Isabella's arm. "You can do it, miss. I can tell that you have good energy."

Isabella laughed. "If you say so."

"Is there anything else that I can get you?"

"No. Thank you very much. I think I will relax for a half hour or so and then I will walk back to meet with my advisor."

Isabella watched out the window for a few seconds as Malee turned around in the golf cart. The view really was better than she'd even imagined—a peaceful and good sign of things to come.

Isabella sat cross-legged on the carpet across from her advisor, Preeda, whom she'd met only moments before. She instantly liked the woman with the long black hair, who had the most stunning and serene presence of anyone Isabella had ever encountered.

Preeda seemed to be listening intently as Isabella answered her questions—wondering how she could possibly remember everything without writing down a word. Yet she had the sense that she was being heard in a way that she'd not been heard before. It was oddly comforting, considering the private things she was telling the woman she'd only just met.

"And would you say that your heart is very open to this experience? Are you willing to trust in yourself and the divine nature that is all around you, Isabella?"

Malee quietly slipped a tray with tea and crackers in between the two women, smiling at Isabella as if to confirm the words her peer was sharing.

"Yes, I'd say so. I mean, I've never really done anything like this before so I'm not sure exactly what to expect—or if it will even be possible for me to meditate, quiet my mind, or whatever is required of me."

Preeda put her hand over Isabella's and Isabella felt the instant warmth coming from her fingers, as if her very touch matched the exact impression that she gave off—one of warmth and genuine kindness. If this was what being mindful and meditative was all about, Isabella was sure that she could benefit from it.

"Isabella, nothing is required. This experience is only for you. We want you to leave here feeling much better than when you arrived. We want you to leave here feeling like you are more of yourself—more of who you are meant to be. If that makes sense?"

The tears were instant. The words could have been the same that she'd read a hundred times from her birth mother's journals. More of who she was meant to be—it seemed so simple, yet she seemed to need constant reminders. She felt both comforted and comfortable with Preeda, though—like she was exactly where she was meant to be.

Preeda reached around behind where she was sitting to pick up a box of tissues. She held it out in front of her so that Isabella could grab one to wipe her eyes. "It's okay. Take your time. It's all okay, Isabella. You tell me only what you want to, and we will be meeting many more times throughout your stay here. There is no hurry."

TWENTY-ONE

Preeda's words to Isabella that first day had stuck with her during her entire stay at the retreat center, and she'd only received more of the same kind and quiet nurturing from everyone that she encountered there, including the monks whom she'd learned so much from.

By the time her final meeting with Preeda had come around—on the last day of her stay there—Isabella felt like a completely new person. Well, not that she'd changed that much—not in ways that were probably noticeable anyway—but she felt lighter and freer than she'd felt in months.

Over the course of her stay, she had opened up to Preeda—about her fears and about her guilt over what she felt had been a betrayal to Thomas. But more importantly, through meditation and what she'd learned from the monks and her talks with her new confidant, she learned what it was to truly accept things.

She could now accept that she'd been operating from a place of fear—a deep fear that she was ultimately going to lose Thomas anyway—whether she stayed in New York or whether she betrayed their relationship when she kissed another man. She was able to quiet her judgments and her fears enough so that she could truly live in the moment and accept that what was meant to happen would happen as long as she lived in a way that was true to herself. And as long as she was honest with Thomas.

She leaned in to give Preeda a big hug. "I can't thank you enough. Truly."

"It's been completely our pleasure. And Isabella, I do hope that we'll see you again soon."

Isabella nodded. She'd already looked into booking one of the villas when Thomas came to visit, thinking that the retreat might be a little much for him, but she thought that he'd love the serenity and beauty of the place just as much as she did.

"We've called for a taxi. He should be along any minute."

"Thank you. Can I ask you one more thing—a favor, and I hope I'm not overstepping my bounds." She leaned in to whisper to her, unfolding her hand enough so that Preeda could see the small object that she held.

Isabella made her way back along the lake to the spot that had become her favorite. It was a small wooden swing, just big enough for three small children or a pair of young lovers. It sat back about two feet from the lake and she'd sat there for hours over the course of the past seven days, contemplating her life and what she wanted her future to be like.

She sat on the swing now and gently took the small bag of ashes out of the small box that always traveled with her for such occasions. She smiled as she thought about all the places throughout Europe where she'd already spread Arianna's ashes. She'd been on this journey with her birth mother since the day she'd met her grandparents and wonderful new extended family in Tuscany—since the day that Lia had first given her the box of items that Arianna had so carefully put together for a daughter she'd never know.

It had been a physical journey to parts unknown but it had also been an intensely emotional and spiritual journey as well, one that Isabella felt confident a young Arianna would have known in a similar way. And Thailand was their first stop together in another part of the world that Arianna had had a huge desire to see.

Isabella gently opened the small bag toward the lake as she said a silent prayer of blessing, letting the wind take the ashes along on their journey. "To Thailand—the 'Land of Smiles' and another stop on our journey together."

TWENTY-TWO

Isabella walked across the floor to check the arrival times again— just to be sure. According to the board, the flight had landed fifteen minutes ago. She walked back over to the waiting area outside of where Thomas would be clearing customs. If she stood in the right spot, she could make out the lines of people placing their luggage on the belts to go through the scan.

She had to smile, thinking about how comfortable she'd become in and out of airports these days. Since her first flight to Thailand only three short months ago, she'd also been to Cambodia and Vietnam. She'd had to leave anyway to secure a longer visa for Thailand, so when Dylan and a few of the others had offered to help her plan a two-week trip, she jumped at the chance to see more of Southeast Asia. Though she'd been more than a little nervous about doing the trip on her own, she was starting to discover just how easy it was to go off and explore, and that there always seemed to be plenty of people around to help her when she had questions or didn't quite know what she was doing.

She stood on her tiptoes, to peek past a gentleman who had stepped in front of her as she waited in the arrival area. She grinned when she spotted Thomas. He was looking down at something in his hands and when he looked back up, she waved to him. Did he see her yet?

Thomas smiled and then waved back at her before grabbing his suitcase off the conveyer belt and heading toward the final exit that would have her in his arms within seconds.

Isabella didn't wait a moment longer once he'd stepped into the arrival area. She ran, jumping into his arms as he dropped his suitcase and held her close. She threw her head back a little so that she could look him in the eyes.

"Hey, you."

"Hey, Iz." He grinned back at her before covering her lips with his for a full minute. "Gosh, it's good to see you."

She smiled back at him, fully enjoying the sensation of being in his arms again. "It's good to see you too. I've missed you so much."

Thomas put her feet back on the ground and reached out to take her hand firmly in his while he picked his suitcase back up with his other hand. "So, shall we?"

"We shall. Wait here. I'll just go get us a taxi."

She walked over to the taxi window, her heart still beating wildly in her chest. She really couldn't believe the day had come. There were reasons to feel sad or homesick with Christmas just around the corner, but Thomas was there with her now. Everything was going to be perfect.

Isabella confirmed the address with the driver as they settled into the backseat of the car. She had a slight flash of panic as she remembered her first arrival—the first time she'd taken a taxi to her Chiang Mai apartment—when she'd met Dylan only three short months ago. It seemed like ages ago, yet the memory of it only reminded her that there were now secrets between her and Thomas. She leaned over to kiss him on the cheek, pushing any thoughts out of her mind that didn't have to do with how ecstatic she was to be with him.

"I can't wait to show you everything. I really think you're going to like it here."

Thomas grinned back at her, lifting his eyebrows in that silly way that she loved. "I can't wait to see your apartment. We may have to have a little rest together before I'm ready to have you play tour guide."

"Are you very tired?"

"Rest is code for—I can't wait to get you alone, my darling. I've been so looking forward to some Izzy snuggle time."

Isabella laughed and then scooted even closer to him on the seat. She grabbed his hand and squeezed it tight as they watched out their opposite windows for a few minutes.

"Well, I can sure tell that I'm not in New York any more. It all looks so different. And yes, I am excited to explore and see everything that you've told me so much about." He leaned down and kissed the top of her head. "But mostly I'm just excited to be here with you."

She rested her head against his shoulder. "It's gonna be great, Thomas."

TWENTY-THREE

Isabella held his hand tight as they walked down one of her favorite streets together. Watching Thomas look around at everything for the first time reminded her of her own arrival and how new and exciting it had all been. She couldn't believe that he was actually there with her now, about to share their first authentic Thai meal together in one of her favorite restaurants.

After the taxi had dropped them off at her apartment, they'd snuggled up together on the sofa for a short nap. Being in Thomas's arms again had felt so completely right to Isabella. She already had pangs of sadness, even thinking about him leaving when his holiday break was over.

As much as everything felt right and the same between them, Isabella thought that Thomas was acting a bit odd. He seemed quieter than normal, but he was probably feeling a bit out of sorts due to the jet lag. This was what she kept telling herself—that she was just being paranoid—because of her own secrets.

She sighed even thinking about it. She was crazy to think that she could keep anything from Thomas. She would tell him what had happened between her and Dylan. She'd go crazy thinking about it until she did. And she'd already made peace with it herself.

Telling Thomas was the right thing to do. But not tonight. Tonight was just going to be about enjoying their reunion.

Thomas elbowed her lightly. "Earth to Iz."

"What? Sorry."

"Yeah, you were a million miles away there. I was just asking you if we're almost to the restaurant. I'm suddenly starving, and I can't wait to try some of this curry that you've been talking about for the past few weeks."

"Oh, it will be worth the wait. Trust me. And it's just one more block, I think."

They settled in at a cozy little corner table at a restaurant that Isabella had been frequenting quite often. The waiter brought them their menus and took their drink orders.

Thomas folded his menu closed. "You know what? I'm just going to have you order everything. Surprise me."

"Are you sure? How spicy do you want it?"

"Oh, you know. Medium—like we have at home."

"Okay, so I'll ask for just a little spice—because their medium here is going to be way too spicy for you."

Thomas reached for her hand across the table. "Sure. Whatever you think."

"Whatever I think, huh?" Isabella winked at him.

"I trust you completely."

Isabella nearly choked on her water as she broke eye contact with him.

"Slow down there. You okay? We haven't even gotten to the spicy stuff yet."

She laughed, thankful that the waiter had returned to take their order. When he'd left she turned her attention back to Thomas, reaching for his hand across the table. "So tell me everything. Tell me about school? Has Biology gotten any easier? Hey, for that matter, when do you get your grades? And I guess we should probably be celebrating the fact that you're done with Biology now, right?"

She grinned at him, having a sudden flashback to their high school days when they'd celebrate after final exams. Which, in reality, meant that they were usually both celebrating the fact that Isabella was able to stop freaking out about them. Thomas never really studied all that much or cared about his own grades, where Isabella seemed to care way too much. At least that's what Thomas used to tell her.

Thomas sighed and kind of half smiled at her. "Yeah, it feels good to be done with exams, that's for sure. Grades should be posted online—I dunno—I think maybe a few days after Christmas, maybe."

"So, have you thought at all about what classes you're going to take next semester? When can you register? You can do it online, right?" She took a sip of her water and waited for Thomas to answer her.

He brushed through his hair with his fingers, looking completely weird and uncomfortable. Something was definitely going on with him—something that was making Isabella feel increasingly more worried. What was he not telling her?

"Iz, can we just please not talk about school right now? I feel like I just finished, and last week was so crazy. It's kinda the last thing I wanna talk about right now, ya know. I mean, I'm not going to lie. It's not been all that great, but everything's going to be fine. I promise, okay?" He smiled at her, and Isabella's heart fell because she knew his forced smile when she saw it.

"Sure. We don't have to talk about anything you don't want to talk about. I want this to be a vacation for you, not something that feels stressful." Did talking to her feel stressful to him now?

Thomas brought her hand up toward his lips to kiss it. "I'm sorry, babe. I think I'm just starting to feel how tired I am from the flight. Of course I want to talk about everything with you."

They were momentarily interrupted by the waiter, who'd begun placing dish after dish of delicious-looking plates of food in front of them on the table.

"Wow, Iz, you ordered enough to feed an army."

Isabella laughed. "Yeah, I might have gone a little overboard. Good thing it tastes just as great warmed up for leftovers the next day."

"I guess so." Thomas began scooping food onto his plate and then straight into his mouth, a few seconds later practically choking as he reached for his water. "Wow, you weren't kidding about the spice. That might take a little getting used to."

"It's really good though, right?"

Thomas nodded. "Iz, sorry about earlier. I didn't mean to hurt your feelings."

"It's okay. I understand, and thank you for saying that. I really do want you to have a nice stress-free vacation. Does it feel weird to you, not being with family for Christmas?"

"No, because I'm with you."

Thomas and Isabella had celebrated Christmases together for as long as she could remember. Typically when they were kids, they'd do the actual holiday with their respective families, but as soon as that was over, they'd get together at the diner, or the movies, or ice-skating, or even sometimes for sleepovers at one another's house.

"How 'bout you?" Thomas asked. "What are your parents doing?"

"Believe it or not, they are actually going on a cruise."

"Wow, glad to hear that they're enjoying their retirement."

Isabella nodded. "Me too. And everyone else will be at the villa —in Tuscany. I promised Lia we'd video chat with them. Don't let me forget.

"Oh, and—now I hope this doesn't stress you out—that fact that I didn't talk to you about it first."

Thomas laughed. "What, Iz? Go on."

"Well, remember that retreat I went to a few months ago—out in the country?"

Thomas nodded his head, his mouth full of food.

"I booked us in for a few nights. Not for the retreat or anything, but in one of the cute little villas they have on the lake there. Uh—for tomorrow night. I hope that's okay. I promise it will be really relaxing."

Thomas made a funny face at her. "Iz, that sounds great. Don't be so worried. Really. I'm happy to do whatever you want to do—whatever you want to show me, I'm game. My only request right now is that we get the check and head back to the apartment. I'm feeling really beat, and I'd rather get a good night's sleep tonight in order to be ready to go tomorrow."

"Sure. Let's get you home and to bed. I'm pretty tired myself."

TWENTY-FOUR

Isabella swung back and forth on the swing by the lake. She and Thomas had arrived at the retreat center a few hours earlier, and already she was feeling more at peace with herself and any weirdness that seemed to be going on with Thomas. It was hard for her to put her finger on it exactly. Things felt the same, yet different somehow. She guessed that it was her own feelings about needing to talk to him—to make good on the promise she'd made when she'd last been here, actually. She'd feel better once everything was out in the open, regardless of the outcome. That's what she was telling herself anyway.

But Thomas had also been acting a little strange. He'd been on his computer a lot more than was typical for him, but she had to remind herself that this new studious Thomas was someone that she needed to get used to. He probably had to take care of some things that had to do with school. What felt like secrecy to Isabella, could very well be the stress of that, which he likely wouldn't want to burden her with.

He'd told her to go on to the lake without him—that he'd join her there shortly.

Isabella took a deep cleansing breath in, just as she'd learned while she'd been on the grounds by the lake doing her meditation weeks ago. She tried to clear her mind and remember all of the healing thoughts that she'd had back then. She had carried much of it with her when she'd left, but it was also very easy to slip back into old ways of thinking. It was something that she constantly had to remind herself of—that everything was just as it was meant to be, including Thomas and his reactions to her—as long as she was being honest with herself and those she loved.

So she'd tell him today. And probably it would be the case that she was far more worried about it than she needed to be. She was almost certain that Thomas would understand about the kiss, once she'd explained everything to him. Well, not that it wouldn't bother him, but in her experience, he really had never been the jealous type before.

Even as she had the thought, though, she knew that it was slightly off. He wasn't just a guy she was dating. He was her one true love. She felt it in her core.

But was she his?

She felt his arms as they came around her shoulders from behind, interrupting her thoughts momentarily. He walked around the front of the swing to sit beside her, then he pulled her over unto his lap as he kissed her full on the lips.

"How are you doing out here? It's so peaceful. I like it a lot."

"Oh, good. I'm glad. I was second-guessing myself after you were so tired last night. But hopefully you can get more good rest during our stay here."

He kissed her again. "Yes, and also more of this."

She laughed. "I'm always up for more of kissing you." His lips were the sweetest thing she'd ever tasted, incomparable to any other kiss she'd ever had. She wanted to burn that thought, that sensation, into every ounce of her being—to remember it forever, for after the time would come that he'd have to leave her.

He pulled her back against his chest and they both sat in easy silence for a few minutes, looking out over the lake, the slight breeze pushing them gently in the swing.

"Thomas, is everything okay? Everything that you had to take care of, I mean?"

"Yeah, everything is fine. Just some loose ends that need to be tied up."

"Why do I get the sense that you're keeping something from me?" She blurted it out before she'd had a chance to think about it. It was bothering her, but then again how dare she push him in that way? When she was the one keeping secrets? She was going to be making things worse but somehow she couldn't stop herself. "I just mean that I can tell something is off. And it's making me feel bad, that's all."

Thomas had pulled back slightly from her and she scooted off his lap so that she could see his eyes. He had a funny look on his face, but it didn't seem bad or guilty, really.

"Thomas, what is it? Please tell me. I'm not going to bug you about school—or about anything—if that's what you're worried about."

Thomas laughed. "Iz, you are so hard to keep secrets from."

She raised her eyebrow. "So, I'm right."

"Well, yes. If you want to put it that way. I have been keeping something from you, and why do you have to be so ridiculously hard to surprise, woman?"

Isabella smiled as the words sunk in.

"Yes, Iz. I'm trying to plan a surprise for you—for Christmas. Can we just leave it at that?"

He was grinning at her and now she felt silly, but so very relieved. "Yes, of course. You know how much I love surprises."

"Yes, I do know, which is why I've been trying to have a few moments to myself today to get something organized." He pulled her to his chest again. "Which hasn't been easy, I might add. Because all I really wanna do is hold you in my arms all day."

His fingers lightly stroked up her arm, causing a shiver to run throughout her entire body.

"You do?" She turned her face slightly so that he could bring his mouth down to hers for a gentle kiss.

"I do."

She sighed. She felt relief for what Thomas had shared with her, but also the dread of what was still to come. She couldn't tell him now. They were both too happy in the moment, and the last thing she wanted was to spoil it. But she was being incredibly selfish in her decision too. She knew that.

TWENTY-FIVE

She stared across the table at Thomas as he finished the last of his dessert. They'd spent a wonderful day together. They'd gone for a long walk, holding hands and kissing every time they stopped. It was like they were a couple of young kids in love, which in actuality they kind of were, she supposed. She grinned when Thomas looked up to catch her staring at him.

"What's that look for? Do I have something on my face?"

"Oh, nothing. I just love you so much and I'm so glad that you're here with me."

He grinned back at her. "That's a big ditto for me, babe. I love you too. You know that. And being here with you like this today— it does remind me of all our time traveling together. And I do miss being with you like that, Iz."

Isabella thought she saw something flash across his face. "Me too. So much. I can't even think about it ending—about you leaving in just a week. I have some ideas for spring break. I was thinking—"

"Iz. Let's just focus on now, okay? There will be plenty of time to talk about spring break later."

Isabella felt her face fall. She didn't like it when he shut her down like that. And it also wasn't typical of their relationship. She was just excited about any time that they'd have together. Usually Thomas was supportive and entertained her desire to talk through things, regardless of how far off in the future they might be. She'd always been a planner. It was something he used to tease her endlessly about when they were younger, but he'd always listened to her.

"Iz, I'm sorry." He reached for her hand across the table.

She was a bundle of emotions all of a sudden; she hadn't realized that she was going to cry until the tears were already falling. It wasn't just about their conversation. It was about the way that she was behaving. She was the one with the secrets. She was the one who was being less than honest with him, and she was suddenly feeling incredibly guilty for that. He didn't deserve it. Thomas deserved to know the truth.

"Honey, why are you crying?"

Thomas was looking at her now with such concern in his eyes —just the way he always had when she was upset. Ever since they were kids, he was always the one to comfort her, to stick up for her when someone wasn't treating her right. He'd always been that person for her, regardless of his own circumstances. Thomas was one of the most unselfish people she knew. It was something that she'd always loved about him. And he would say the same about her, but would he still?

"Iz, you know that you can tell me anything. And I'm sorry if I hurt your feelings."

He squeezed her hand and she pulled it away into her lap. *Just say it, Iz.* She looked up at him and took a deep breath in before she spoke. "Thomas, I've done something. And I've not been honest with you." She was trying not to cry, but the look of confusion that she saw on his face only made her tears fall more.

"Okay. What is it? You're freaking me out a little bit." He took a drink of his wine and then put it back on the table as he waited for Isabella to speak.

Just say it. She hated herself now. She'd been doing her best to push everything aside for weeks and now here she was—faced with the moment of truth, faced with the look on Thomas's face, which wasn't going to get any better in the next few minutes.

"Thomas, I didn't mean for it to happen and it didn't mean anything at all, but I kissed a guy." She looked down at her hands. "It was a while ago—just when I first arrived, actually, and nothing ever happened beyond that one kiss. That was all and it never happened again. And I've regretted it every day since then. I'd had a few wines and it was my fault because I hadn't told him about you at that point. It was just really stupid." She finally looked at him. "I'm so sorry, Thomas. You know I would never do anything to hurt you."

He was quiet, and she didn't miss the look of hurt in his eyes. She had hurt him. It was crazy to think otherwise. Had it been reversed and it was him sharing such a thing with her, she would have been devastated. It had been a betrayal, and she could see that clear as anything on his face now as he didn't even look at her.

"Thomas, please say something." She reached for his hand, but he yanked it away.

"What, Isabella? What do you expect me to say to that? I mean, I'm feeling a little shocked right now, I suppose. Of all the things I expected you might say to me—of all the reasons I thought you might be crying..." He didn't finish his sentence as his hands went up through his hair, a gesture of discomfort that Isabella knew all too well. "Who was it, Iz?"

His question took her by surprise for some reason, but it wasn't out of line. For a brief second she thought about saying that it had been a random traveler, someone just passing through town, but the lie wasn't a better answer, really. And she needed to tell the truth. Otherwise what was the whole point of the confession in the first place?

"Iz?"

She took a deep breath. She'd told Thomas about Dylan when she'd first arrived and she'd also continued talking about the fact that she sometimes hung out with him and a group of friends at the cafes. But she never went out with Dylan alone. Not since the night that the kiss had happened. But what would Thomas think about it?

Thomas sighed. "Just tell me. Look, nothing you could say is going to be any worse, right? Iz? I mean I hope that it's true that nothing else happened. Frankly, I can't even believe that we're having this conversation right now."

"I know. Okay. It was Dylan. I've talked about him to you. I know it sounds kinda weird but we really are just friends. Nothing else has ever happened between us—nothing ever would. Thomas, I just made a mistake. I'm so sorry." She was trying to fight her tears. She knew that Thomas hated to see her cry and it didn't seem fair to do that to him now. She needed to give him his space so that he could process what she'd just told him.

Thomas stood up, reached into his pocket, and laid some cash down on the table. "I need to go for a walk. I'm going to ask them out front to escort you back to the villa."

Isabella stood up too and tried to put her arms around his neck, but he gently pushed her away.

"Iz, please. I just need to get some air—to clear my head. I'll come back."

"Promise?" *What if he doesn't come back?* She shouldn't have told him.

As he nodded his head in reply, he looked her in the eye for the first time since she'd told him her secret. She saw that he was holding back tears himself. She hated that she'd caused that hurt or anger or whatever it was that he was feeling toward her. She had to make him understand. He just had to forgive her.

He turned and walked away toward the path by the lake, and Isabella sat back down in her chair. She hoped that Thomas would let her explain further—that he'd listen to everything she'd learned since that night. But she had to give him his space. Thomas would make his own decisions, and she'd learn to live with them if he no longer wanted her in his life. As hard as it was, she could accept that now. But that didn't stop the gnawing fear she had that she was about to lose her best friend and the love of her life.

TWENTY-SIX

Isabella waited for Thomas to join her out on their balcony for breakfast. It was so peaceful there, overlooking the lake. The calm water almost seemed to taunt her, for her night had been restless and without much sleep at all.

She'd waited up for hours after dinner, hoping that Thomas would come back and want to talk. She could see him sitting out there—by the water—right before she finally crawled in bed. It was all she could do to keep from going to him, but she'd promised herself that she'd wait until he was ready.

And when he'd come in quietly, about an hour after that, she'd felt his lips light on her cheek right before he turned off the light to go to bed. She'd turned and reached up to put her hands around his neck, desperate to feel his face next to her, but he'd gently removed her hands and whispered that they'd talk in the morning. And that he loved her.

She took a sip of her coffee and tried to calm her beating heart. He'd given her the words she'd longed to hear. Thomas was good about not playing games, about not leaving her hanging. Even when they'd argue during their younger days—and they'd had days of not speaking to one another, to be sure—it was always Thomas who called late at night, right before he went to bed. "Let's be done being mad now, Iz, okay?" he'd say and Isabella would laugh into the phone. And the next day everything would be back to normal, the past forgotten, their friendship the most important thing always when it came to petty arguments.

Isabella took a big gulp of fresh air. But this wasn't a petty argument and there was much more to lose than when they'd been twelve years old.

Finally, when Isabella thought she couldn't stand it another minute, she saw Thomas coming out of the bathroom, freshly shaven and looking handsome in the plush robe that had been provided by the villa. He let room service in, gesturing to the balcony as he waited to see him out again.

Once the waiter had gone, he sat across from Isabella at the table. Finally she could look into his eyes and search for the reassurance that she was desperate for.

She cleared her throat, nervous and unsure of where to begin. "Thomas, I—I don't know exactly what to say, but I need you to know how sorry I am. I'm sorry that I hurt you and I hope we can talk about it—that I can explain a little bit more to you. I just—I think maybe I can help you to feel a little better, if that makes any sense."

He just looked at her. He didn't look angry or sad exactly, but his silence was unnerving. It wasn't like him to not talk to her when something was bothering him, and it was almost as if she could see the wheels turning silently in his head with thoughts that he didn't intend to share with her—not anytime soon, anyway.

"Thomas, please. Won't you please tell me what you're thinking? I know what I told you last night must have come as a shock to you, but we have to talk about it." She was reaching for words now, desperate to get him to tell her what was on his mind. "Look, it's certainly not like you to be jealous. Let's not forget that we've known one another through several relationships in the past—or I've known you through several of your relationships, I should say.

I know you're not exactly the jealous type—or at least you've not been before."

Isabella's head jerked up at the sound of Thomas putting his fork down with a clatter against his plate. She saw the flash of anger across his face just before he spoke in what seemed like carefully selected words.

"Is that what you think? That I could possibly stand the thought of you being in another guy's arms—kissing another guy the way that you kiss me? Please tell me that you see the difference here. Because if you don't know by now how much I love you— that you're not just another girl that I've been dating, Iz—well, I guess that's what would have me more confused than anything." He sighed and ran his fingers through his hair. "If you only knew..."

His voice trailed off and Isabella felt slightly shocked at his outburst, but at least they were talking now.

"If I only knew what?" She'd whispered the question and when he looked at her intently, she could see that there was a lot he wasn't saying. She hated that she'd caused the confusion that she could see so clearly in his eyes. It was the one thing she had to convince him of—that he hadn't been wrong to love her, to trust her.

"I dunno, Iz. I'm just so confused." He reached over and took her hand, and she was so grateful for his touch that it was all she could do to keep from bursting into tears. He took a deep breath. "Okay, I'm listening now. Please help me to understand."

They talked for hours out on the balcony, Isabella holding nothing back as she confessed her insecurities and the fear that she had that he would leave her eventually—that regardless of whether she was living in New York or traveling, he'd come to discover that his feelings for her weren't as strong as what she felt for him.

And she also told Thomas everything that she'd left out earlier about her experience at the resort center—that the kiss hadn't really been about Dylan, but more about her own reassurance and need to mask some of the feelings of loneliness that she'd been having when she first arrived. She told him the truth in that she and Dylan were friends—that they didn't hang out alone together and that he wasn't the bad guy in the situation. But she also told Thomas that she would stop hanging out with Dylan altogether if it made him uncomfortable.

Thomas stood up and then reached out his hands to pull Isabella from her chair. He pulled her over to him, wrapping his arms around her, as he hugged her close.

She'd been longing to be held by him, so much so that she couldn't hold her tears back any longer. She wept into his chest and finally tilted her head back just a little so that she could look him in the eye. "Thomas, I love you so much."

He leaned in slightly to kiss her on the forehead.

She took a breath and looked up at him again. "Please say that you can forgive me."

He looked back at her and she thought some of the confusion had left his face—some, but maybe not all. It would probably take some time. She had to be willing to accept that and just reassure him that her words were true.

He kissed her gently on the lips. "I do forgive you. I may not agree with everything that you allowed to happen, but I do forgive you, Iz. And more importantly, I love you—more than anything— and I—I almost feel as if I owe you an apology. If I've ever done anything to make you doubt that—doubt my love for—"

She stopped him with her lips on his and their kiss intensified almost immediately. She looked up at him when their kiss broke. "You have nothing to apologize for. You've never given me a reason to doubt your feelings for me and I'm sorry that I ever did. I honestly think I've moved on from those old insecurities. Thomas, having you in my life has been the best thing that's ever happened to me. I'd be so shattered if I ever lost you." She shuddered even thinking about it, and once more he pulled her into that hug of security that she'd known for so much of her life.

"Good thing that you're stuck with me then." He laughed and Isabella felt instant relief. They were going to be okay. She knew that now.

She grinned at him as he grabbed her hand, making a gesture that it was time for them to go inside for some privacy.

"So, does this mean that I still get my Christmas surprise?" She was laughing when she asked the question and Thomas laughed too, but there was something about his expression that made her wish she hadn't joked about it.

"Oh, you'll get something for Christmas, don't you worry about that." He blew her a kiss from across the room. "Now come over here on the sofa with me so that I can assure you once again of my love for you."

She laughed at the way he'd sprawled himself across the sofa and she crossed the room, all thoughts of Christmas and Dylan and anything unrelated to being in Thomas's arms vanishing from her mind.

TWENTY-SEVEN

Isabella sipped her latte as she listened to Thomas practice his Thai. He had asked her to help him, which she found rather hysterical, considering she had mastered exactly three phrases. But she had to give him credit for trying. He had a few apps loaded on his phone, a small English-Thai dictionary in his pocket, and he always attempted to speak to the locals that they interacted with. People did seem to appreciate the effort, even though pretty much everyone there seemed to speak a fair bit of English—or at least those who came into contact with the many tourists did.

She and Thomas had been having such a great morning together. They'd returned from the retreat center the night before and after the talk they'd had there, Isabella felt that things were back to being almost normal again. Well, she felt like things were a lot better, but there was still something a little off about the way Thomas was acting—slightly more reserved than normal—but she really didn't feel that she could say anything else about it. She just needed to give him some time.

That morning she'd taken him into the old part of town. They'd started with a walk around the moat and then a wander around the morning market, which was something that Isabella loved to do.

The first time that she'd ventured out in the early morning, she'd been mesmerized by the city waking up around her. The monks walking barefoot in the streets captivated her as she watched the locals place their gifts of food into the open bowls that they carried, followed by a blessing from the monk that she never tired of watching. It was all so completely different to anything she'd ever known back home.

When they'd chosen the cafe along a quiet street in the center of old town, she was reminded that she felt slightly nervous about running into Dylan in her own neighborhood. So far, they hadn't, but she knew that it was just a matter of time whenever they'd go out there. But here, across town, she didn't think there was a chance of running into anyone she knew.

No sooner had she had the thought than she looked over toward the door of the cafe to see Dylan entering. What were the chances? She felt her whole body tense. Should she not say anything and somehow try to convince Thomas that it was time to go—and out the back way, at that?

But she was never good at hiding how she was feeling. Thomas had always teased her about wearing her heart on her sleeve.

"Iz, what's wrong? You look like you've just seen a ghost. As in, your face is literally drained of color. Are you okay, babe?" He reached across the table for her hand.

No, she wouldn't not tell him. No more secrets. Only the truth from now on. She gestured toward the counter where Dylan was placing his order. He hadn't seen her yet. There was still time to walk out through the patio.

"Dylan just walked in."

"Oh."

She saw his eyes go immediately to where Dylan was standing, his back still to them.

"It's so weird, because we're all the way across town and I've never heard him mention this place. Anyway, should we go, Thomas? I don't want things to be weird or uncomfortable for you."

"No. Not yet. Iz, actually I'd like to meet him."

He squeezed her hand as if to assure her that it was going to be alright, but Isabella felt like she was going to throw up any minute. Before she could try to change Thomas's mind, Dylan was walking toward them, a big smile on his face.

"Hi, Bella. Feels like it's been forever since I've run into you." He looked over at Thomas, who had stood up from the table.

"Dylan, this is Thomas. He's here visiting for Christmas." She turned slightly toward Thomas. "Thomas, Dylan."

Dylan stuck his hand out to shake the one that Thomas had offered him. "Great to meet you, Thomas, and welcome to Thailand. I hope that you've been enjoying your time here."

Isabella was sure that Dylan must be feeling at least a little bit uncomfortable. Thomas's visit hadn't come up the last time that she'd seen him out, so he was probably feeling unsure about what Thomas knew about their past encounter.

Thomas shook Dylan's hand and remained cordial. Isabella wouldn't have expected anything less from him, really—not without good reason. And Dylan, always the gentleman, was not going to give him a reason to dislike him—well, other than the fact that he'd shared one kiss with his girlfriend. But Thomas was a reasonable guy, and with Dylan not knowing about her boyfriend, he could hardly be faulted for a mistake that had rested completely on Isabella's shoulders.

"Good to meet you too." Thomas remained standing.

"Well, I'll let you two get back to your conversation." Dylan held up his notebook. "I've just come to enjoy the outdoor patio here while I do a little work."

"Can I have a word with you, if you don't mind?" Thomas said.

Dylan nodded and the two walked out the door to a corner of the patio.

Isabella's heart beat rapidly as she watched them out the window. So far, the conversation didn't look heated or anything. Knowing Thomas, he probably wanted to just put it out there that he knew about what had happened—clear the air, so to speak—and possibly to remind Dylan of what Isabella had told him about the two of them agreeing not to spend time alone together.

She let out a breath as she saw the two of them smile at one another and shake hands again, Thomas with one hand on Dylan's shoulder in a friendly gesture before he turned to walk back into the coffee shop.

He sat down across from her, not saying anything for a full minute as he picked up his coffee and seemed to carry on with his language-learning app.

"Thomas?"

"Yeah?" He looked over at her.

"Well? Aren't you going to tell me what that was all about? Is everything okay?"

"Sure. Everything's fine."

"Thomas!"

He laughed and grabbed her hand. "Okay, okay. I'm just teasing you. And hey, you do deserve at least to be teased by me for —oh, I don't know—maybe the next five years or so."

"Touché." She wrinkled her nose at him. But at least he was joking about it. That had to be a good sign.

"So, I just wanted to let Dylan know that I was aware of what had happened between the two of you."

Isabella felt his body tense as he talked about it. She knew that even though Thomas was teasing her—and she did believe that he'd forgiven her—it still probably stung for him to think about it —let alone to talk about it with Dylan.

"Oh, okay."

"And, as much as I hate to admit it, he does seem like a good guy. He apologized and said that had he known about me, nothing would have happened."

Isabella nodded. "Good. So that's over, then. We won't have to worry about any awkward run-ins." She was ready to change the subject and guessed that Thomas would be too. "Are you finished with your studying, then? I'd really like to discuss the rest of our time together. There's a few places that I've not been to yet because I thought maybe you'd enjoy them too."

"Iz, can we talk about that later? I mean, I know you like to plan and everything but let's just take it one day at a time, okay?"

There was that look again. It was odd—not angry or anything, but like he was getting ready to shut down the conversation. She was trying not to be paranoid, but it sure felt like he didn't want to be making any plans with her. Maybe he was just trying to keep things comfortable until it was time for him to fly back home. The thought horrified her.

"Okay, but will you at least give me an idea about what we're doing for Christmas? Do you need me to plan anything? Make any reservations? Are we exchanging gifts, because if we are, I haven't gotten you anything yet." She laughed lightly.

"Soon. I promise. And no. Don't worry about a gift for me. You are gift enough, my love." He grinned.

There he was. Her sweet, goofy Thomas. But he really was driving her a little crazy with this non-planning attitude all of a sudden. "Alrighty then, whatever you say."

"Whatever I say, huh?" Thomas raised his eyebrows, which made her laugh.

"Yeah, yeah." She stood up from the table. "So, did you want to check out one more temple before we head back? There's a really pretty one just down the block from here, I think."

Thomas looked at the time on his phone. "Actually, if you don't mind, I think I'm ready to head back. I have a few more things I need to take care of."

"A few more secret things?" Isabella wrinkled her nose as she asked the question.

"Iz, you really don't like when I keep anything from you, do you? Even if it's a surprise, I mean?"

"No, I guess not. Well, not if you put it like that."

He stood up and pulled her to him. "Iz, I think you're going to like it—the surprise. Can you just trust me?"

She reached up to give him a quick kiss on the lips. "Yes, I do trust you. And I love you."

"Good. Iz?"

"Yeah?"

He kissed her on the forehead before he took her hand in his. "I trust you too."

TWENTY-EIGHT

Isabella adjusted her earbuds as she pulled up the video app on her computer. She really needed to talk to Nina.

She'd sent a note off to Jemma, who was busy with everyone in Tuscany, but she'd promised that she and Thomas would be calling in for Christmas at some point.

As soon as they'd gotten back to the apartment, Thomas had packed up his computer and taken off, saying he was going to go to a cafe for a couple of hours.

Isabella went back and forth between wondering if he really was being secretive about her so-called Christmas surprise or if he, in fact, had a secret girlfriend back home. She didn't really think that was the case, but she did wonder if something was going on that she wasn't really going to ever be privy to. Thomas still hadn't wanted to talk about school with her and there were other topics as well that he'd shied away from ever since he'd arrived.

Her thoughts were interrupted when she saw that her call to Nina was connecting. Seconds later, her friend's face filled her computer screen.

"Hey, you. I've been thinking about you and wondering how

everything's going. Have you been having a good time with Thomas?"

"Hi, Nina. Oh, I'm so glad you're able to chat. Yes, it's been fun having Thomas here and...well, I have a lot to fill you in on, really. But first I want to hear how you're doing. And where are you? Still in Italy?"

"Yes, I'm in Rome now—not a new place for me, but I never tire of this city. There's so much to do and I have a few friends here, so I thought I'd come for a few weeks."

"And then?"

"Well, I've been wanting to ask you what your plans are actually. I've been thinking about Thailand a lot—or maybe somewhere else in Southeast Asia. Do you know what your plans are for after Christmas?"

"No. Not yet. I do really love Chiang Mai, though, so I guess in the back of my mind, I'm thinking of doing another trip somewhere to get a visa and then settling back in here to finish my current book. I definitely agree with your thoughts about getting work done here. It's an easy place for that. Oh, and of course I'd love it if you were here too!"

"Well, let's keep one another posted then about our plans. Now tell me everything. Tell me about Thomas, but we haven't really talked since right before your retreat and I want to hear all about that too."

Isabella had only sent Nina a few quick and rather generic e-mails about her time at the retreat center and she hadn't told her anything about what had happened between her and Dylan. At the time she'd felt ashamed, but now that she was on the other side of everything—now that Thomas knew—she decided to open up to her friend about it. It would be good to get another's woman's perspective. Nina could help remind Isabella of the things that she'd learned at the retreat center about trust and being in the present instead of worrying about the future so much.

Isabella took a deep breath. "Okay, have you got a few minutes? I guess I have a lot to fill you in on."

Over the next thirty minutes or so, Isabella proceeded to tell Nina everything. She surprised herself in that she left nothing out and was also able to relay it all without tears. Nina was a good listener, taking it all in without interruption. Isabella eventually finished by expressing her feelings about whatever secret things Thomas had been doing on his computer and phone pretty much since he'd been there.

"Wow. I guess you did have a lot to tell me. But it sure sounds like you're handing things okay—emotionally, I mean. I'm proud of you for that."

"Trust me, had I talked to you right after everything happened with Dylan, you would have been dealing with a basket case." Isabella laughed lightly. "I was seriously a mess."

"Well, it sounds like your retreat was good timing, then. I'm glad that you found it so helpful. I think it's the perfect thing to do in that part of the world. So much of the environment and spirituality of the place is conducive to that kind of personal growth."

"I agree, and if I decide to stay, I'll definitely be going back for another session. So, what do you think about Thomas? Am I just being paranoid? I mean, I can't really get too worked up when he keeps saying that he's sorting things out back home—whatever that means." Isabella couldn't help rolling her eyes. "Well, and then there's this whole official secret Christmas surprise." Isabella did air quotes around the words "secret Christmas surprise."

Nina laughed. "Bella."

"I know, I know. I'm being a jerk. Just because I've been keeping secrets from him doesn't mean that he's got some big dark one that's going to tear my heart to shreds."

Nina smiled. "No, it doesn't. Thomas loves you. It sounds like he forgives you and wants to move past everything, so maybe you just need to give him a break—at least until after Christmas, right?"

"Yes. You're right, of course. It's my old nature creeping in—that need to know absolutely everything that is happening for the next year or so." Isabella laughed.

"Well, from what you've told me, you and Thomas have been through it all together, so if that's true, I'm sure that he must be pretty used to it by now."

Isabella smiled. Nina's words hit a truth that she hadn't been allowing herself to think about. Thomas did know her—better than anyone. He'd seen the changes and growth in her over the past year, but he'd also been there for her for every year prior to that. And if she believed him—and she did—he'd loved her even back then—not that it was the kind of love a young boy would confess to, but it was a genuine acceptance of a girl whose heart he'd stolen years ago.

Isabella heard the door open, and minutes later Thomas was standing next to her looking down at the computer screen.

"Speak of the devil," Nina said.

Isabella laughed as she looked up at Thomas. "Only good things."

"I'm sure." Thomas bent down to give Isabella a quick kiss on the lips before he looked back to her computer screen. "Hey Nina. How's Italy?"

"Italy is—well, you know—beautiful food, beautiful language, beautiful men..." Nina laughed, as did Thomas.

"So, in one word—beautiful."

"*Sì.*"

"Okay, I'll let you two finish your call." He turned toward Isabella from the doorway. "I'll be out on the balcony, babe."

Isabella nodded and then turned her attention back to Nina. "It's been so good talking to you. Let's do it again soon. And thanks for your always great advice."

"You're welcome any time. Oh, and I was going to say too—about the waiting."

"Yes?"

"I was just going to encourage you that if it's really bothering you so much, you should just bring it up again. I'm sure it's better for your relationship not to hide how you're feeling from him. Well, that's something I was *not* good at myself, so I think it's worth mentioning." Nina winked. "But you two will figure it all out. I have confidence in that. And also, who the heck am I to be giving relationship advice?"

They both laughed.

"You're my good friend who cares about me, that's who. Okay, Nina. Bye for now. Enjoy Rome."

Isabella clicked off the video app and closed her computer. She always felt better after talking to Nina. There was something about her that was both calming and invigorating.

Yes, she'd try to calm her own weird feelings and just enjoy the time that she and Thomas had together. The days were ticking away and she could already feel the dread of his leaving coming soon enough. She certainly wanted to enjoy and embrace every minute that they had together in the meantime. Thomas deserved that. They both deserved that.

TWENTY-NINE

Isabella stopped by the fridge to grab a couple of Cokes and then headed toward the balcony. She could hear Thomas talking through the open window in the living room and without her meaning to eavesdrop, his words stopped her in her tracks just short of the door to the outside.

"Yes, that's fine. Feel free to just move my clothes to the other closet...That's right." He laughed. "Yes, help yourself to anything in the fridge."

Without thinking, Isabella burst out onto the balcony.

"Thomas, you need to tell me what is going on."

Thomas looked up, his face showing the shock of suddenly seeing Isabella standing there beside him. "Okay, I gotta go. Yes, I'll e-mail that to you. Bye." He clicked off the phone and reached for Isabella's hand. "Iz, what's going on?"

Isabella pulled her hand away from him as she sat down in the chair. "I'm asking *you*—what's going on? I heard you, Thomas, so just tell me. Please." Her heart was still racing and she had no idea what he could possibly tell her that was going to make her feel any better. It sure sounded to her like Thomas had a woman moving into his apartment while he was gone. How could he do that to her? Let her think that everything was okay and all the while...Her suspicions about all his secrecy had been right after all.

"Iz, what did you hear? Or what do you think that you heard? Because I can promise you that you absolutely have the wrong idea."

"Well, I think you have a girlfriend back in New York—why you would bother coming here to be with me, I don't know—and it sure sounds like she's moving into your apartment." Isabella looked up at him with the tears flowing down her face. "How could you, Thomas?"

But the look on Thomas's face was not the look of someone who had been caught cheating. It was a look she knew well—slightly teasing, slightly perplexed.

"Iz, are you serious? Do you really believe that?"

"Then tell me, Thomas. Tell me I'm wrong."

Thomas pulled her into his lap, despite her objection. He carefully wiped away the wetness under her eyes with his fingers, all the while giving her a funny look.

"Well, my love, in fact, you are wrong. The person I was talking to just now is a friend of mine from school—Kyle is *his* name. And he's staying at my apartment while I'm away."

Isabella felt instant relief and instant shame all at the same time. "Really?"

"Really." Thomas nodded, then gently pushed a few strands of her hair behind one ear. "But now the question I have for you, my dear, is why would you even jump to that conclusion? I thought we just spent a whole lot of time talking about trust, our relationship, and how much I love you. Do you really think I would do that to you?"

Isabella shook her head and put her hands around his neck. "No. I don't think you would. And I'm sorry. I don't know what's gotten into me, but—"

"But what?"

Isabella did feel relieved at his words and she did believe him, but if she was being honest with herself, she was feeling annoyed because of whatever Thomas had been doing and not telling her about. Why hadn't he bothered to mention that he had a friend staying at his apartment in the first place? It wasn't like him, and she did need to get to the bottom of it or she was going to drive herself crazy over thinking everything.

"Well, you have been acting so secretive and I just don't get why you're not sharing things with me. The fact that you have someone staying at your place, this big Christmas surprise—which I might add is coming up in just three days, you know. I dunno. And other things too. I just notice that there's a lot of things that you don't seem to be sharing with me. And it's bothering me, Thomas. A lot. I just—I'm not trying to nag you. I just need to be honest about it."

Thomas seemed to be studying her, which made her slightly uncomfortable. "What, Thomas? Do you think I'm crazy?"

He kissed her on the nose. "No. I don't think you're crazy. Well, not in a bad way." He grinned at her and stuck his finger lightly in the ticklish spot in her side. "I guess I can see how things could look a little strange. But Iz?"

"Yeah?"

"Do you trust me? I mean, this is important, right?"

Thomas wasn't teasing her any more. She felt the change in his voice. It was a serious question. She stood up from his lap and sat back down in the chair next to him. Thomas turned the chair with her in it so that they were facing one another, knee to knee. He took her hands in his and looked her in the eyes.

"Iz, we do trust one another, don't we? Even after what happened—what you shared with me about Dylan—I do trust you. You know that, right? I believe in you—in the love that we have for one another. But Iz, I gotta know that you believe in me like that too."

Isabella thought it was almost the most serious she'd ever seen him. She felt the weight of the question he was asking her.

"Yes. I do trust you. You've never given me a reason not to and I'm sorry if I seem to be looking for a reason lately." She squeezed his hands. "I'm going to stop doing that now. I promise."

Thomas grinned. "Good." He leaned in and kissed her on the lips. "Now would you like me to put you out of your misery and tell you about the fantastic surprise I've planned for you for Christmas?"

Isabella grinned. "Yes, please."

"Well, what if I said that I've arranged a very romantic Christmas getaway for us in Bali?"

"Oh, Thomas, really?" Isabella got up quickly and placed herself right back down in his lap, throwing her hands around his neck. "I've been dying to go there."

"I know you have." He kissed her gently on the lips. "Me too, and now we'll go there together."

"When? When are we leaving?"

"The day after tomorrow—in the morning. And you don't have to worry about a thing. I've got everything organized."

Isabella kissed him again. "I'm sorry for doubting you. I can't believe that I ever did. And you must have been so annoyed with me as you were planning everything."

"Well, I'm not going to lie. I nearly canceled everything a few times."

Isabella's eyebrow shot up in reaction to his words.

Thomas laughed. "I'm kidding. I figured you'd be surprised when I told you and that it would all be worth it in the end."

"So worth it. Oh, I can't wait, Thomas. This is going to be the best Christmas."

"Yes, I think it is." He winked at her right before he hugged her tighter.

THIRTY

Isabella squeezed Thomas's hand as she looked out the window of the car he'd hired to pick them up at the airport in Denpasar. They were nearing the end of a long drive that would have them at their destination very soon.

She looked over at Thomas, who seemed to be enjoying the view out the window as much as she was. "I can't believe we're actually in Bali."

"I know. Me too. How many times have we talked about coming here?"

She leaned over to kiss him on the cheek.

Thomas laughed. "What was that for?"

"Thank you. For this—for putting up with my craziness the last few days—just for everything."

Isabella had been feeling insanely happy—and relieved. Ever since she and Thomas had had their big talk a few days ago, she'd felt a huge weight lift from her shoulders. She'd become the old her again and she knew that Thomas had felt that too. She still had some questions in her mind. She still noticed the quick phone calls and the time that Thomas spent checking his e-mail—which was more than usual for him—but she'd decided to trust him that everything was fine.

And they'd had so much fun the day before in Chiang Mai—playing tourists—checking out the temples and markets, and wandering around the twisty little streets of the old city. In the afternoon, Thomas had rented a motorbike and they'd gone up to Doi Suthep just before sunset. The view of the city below did not disappoint, and they both agreed that they'd like to come back again after they returned from Bali.

Thomas was looking at her, studying her, as he seemed to be doing a lot in the past few days.

"Iz, you don't have to keep thanking me." He was teasing her. "I enjoy seeing you so happy." He reached out and put her hair back behind her shoulder. "You're always beautiful, but that smile—I love it when you smile."

How was it that he could still make her blush like a twelve-year-old girl? Way before she'd ever realized her crush on her best friend, he'd always showered her with compliments and had a way of making her feel good about herself.

"Well, you make me extremely happy." She was thoughtful. "Thomas?"

"Yeah?"

"You know that it's not about the surprise or the gifts or anything to do with money, don't you? I mean, I'd be with you if we were living in a tent somewhere without electricity."

Thomas feigned a look of shock. "Oh, really?"

Isabella laughed. "Okay, maybe not a tent exactly, but my point is that I'm happiest when we're together, no matter where we are or what we're doing. I mean we're so lucky—I know that—to have everything that we have, but none of that matters to me without you."

Thomas smiled before he leaned in to kiss her deeply.

Moments later, as she looked out her window, they ascended a small hill to arrive at the most beautiful villa she'd ever seen.

"Thomas. Wow!"

"Wow is right. It looks just like the pictures."

They pulled up into the circular driveway, and a man and woman were immediately out the front door to greet them and take their bags.

"Is it a room or—Thomas, you didn't rent the whole place, did you?"

"I did. Merry Christmas, babe."

Isabella threw her arms around him and he picked her up to give her a big kiss.

"Now, shall we go inside to check it out? I think I'll tell the driver to come back in a few hours. That way we can have a little rest before we go exploring. Sound good?"

Isabella grabbed his hand and started walking toward the entrance. "That sounds perfect."

The sound of Thomas's light snoring made her smile. He'd been asleep for a good hour and she tried not to make too much noise as she worked to unpack her suitcase. Already, Isabella felt relaxed and happy as she thought about their next four days on the island. She'd decided that she wouldn't do any work unless she was absolutely struck with something that she had to write. Thomas would be leaving only two days after they returned to Thailand, and she wanted to spend every minute that they had left together.

She carefully picked up the little box that contained a small amount of Arianna's ashes that she'd almost forgotten to pack. She needed to update the map; now she could add Indonesia to the list of Southeast Asian countries that she'd been to. Bali had most certainly been on Arianna's list.

She saw Thomas watching her out of the corner of her eye as she placed the box in the drawer of the nightstand beside her bed.

He smiled at her as he scooted over to the other side of the bed. "How's it been, Iz?" He nodded his head in the direction of the drawer she'd just closed. "With the ashes? Does it still make you sad?"

Isabella sat down on the edge of the bed and turned to look at him lying there beside her. "You know, it doesn't make me sad. Not really. Mostly it makes me feel closer to her." She looked down, wondering if her words were going to make any sense to him.

He reached out and pulled her back gently against the pillow as he turned on his side to look at her. "I think that's wonderful, Iz." He leaned over and gave her a quick kiss.

She smiled at his words and his kiss. "It's like somehow I've gotten to know her more and more through my own travels and —" Isabella hadn't shared her most recent thoughts about Arianna with anyone—not even Thomas.

"And?" He reached out and rubbed the length of her arm with gentle fingers. The touch was so sweet, so loving, that Isabella felt herself on the verge of tears.

She looked into his eyes for only a moment before she spoke. "And sometimes I talk to her. In that moment, when the breeze lifts her ashes out of my hand, I feel like she's whispering to me— like she's there with me, thanking me for bringing her on this journey." She reached for Thomas's hand, giving it a squeeze. "I don't know if I'm explaining it very well. I probably sound a bit nuts, huh?"

Thomas kissed her on the lips. "No. You're explaining it perfectly—beautifully. It's something very special and I'm glad that you've had that with her—that you'll keep having that."

Isabella nodded.

"Do you want to bring it with us tonight? I'm sure we can find a pretty spot by the water."

"Yeah, I will, but there's no pressure. I've really been trying to trust my instinct about the right location and time. I'm sure we'll be able to find the perfect spot here in Bali." She stood up from the bed and reached for Thomas's hand. "Speaking of perfect spots,

Thomas you have to check out the rooftop. You're not going to believe the view from up there."

Thomas let her pull him up from the bed. He checked his phone on the nightstand. "Sure, we have about an hour before our driver comes to pick us up. I figure we'll explore a bit of the area, maybe go for a walk on the beach, and then go to one of those little beach restaurants we passed on the way here. Something casual for tonight I think would be fun."

Isabella grinned. "I like it when you're in charge."

Thomas raised his eyebrows and swatted her lightly on the behind. "Is that so?"

Isabella laughed as she took off running out of the room with Thomas chasing after her.

THIRTY-ONE

Isabella combed through her wet hair while looking in the bathroom mirror. It had been such a magical two days in Bali. They'd gone for long walks on the beach and snorkeled in clear water full of fish and coral. She and Thomas had been talking—and connecting—on a deeper level than they ever had before, and everything about it was comforting to her.

And now Thomas was taking her somewhere special for Christmas dinner. She missed her parents and her whole family in Tuscany, of course, but somehow it felt just right that she and Thomas should spend the holiday alone together in such a magical part of the world.

She finished drying off and wrapped the thick plush bathrobe around her. She opened the door quietly and before she stepped out into the bedroom, she could see Thomas where he stood outside on the balcony. She felt a lump in her throat at the sight of him. When had he become so handsome to her? His profile was perfect and she didn't miss the fact that he was wearing a suit. She smiled. Where had he gotten a suit?

She walked out into the bedroom, just as he turned to walk toward her.

"Thomas, what's going on around here?" She laughed. "You certainly look handsome—but where did the suit come from? I'm quite sure that you didn't have that packed with you. Now I'm also not sure that I have the appropriate attire for tonight's— apparently quite fancy—dinner." She was laughing but the reality was that she didn't have anything with her to match how dressed-up Thomas was for the occasion.

Thomas grinned at her and reached down by the side of the bed to bring up a large white box with a giant red bow. "Merry Christmas, Iz." He brought it around to the other side of the bed, setting it down and then pulling her in for a big hug.

"Thomas! But I didn't get you anything. I thought we said—"

"Shh. Just open it."

Isabella lifted the cover off the box and pulled the tissue paper back to reveal the most gorgeous deep red fabric. She lifted it out and held it at arm's length to admire the most beautiful dress she'd ever seen. "Oh, Thomas, it's so gorgeous. Where on earth—how— where did this come from?" Isabella was both pleasantly surprised and entirely confused.

Thomas smiled. "Let's just say that you can finally put your mind at ease as to what some of my phones calls have been about."

"Ahh, I see." And more of the pieces started to come together in Isabella's head, allowing her to feel completely content in a single moment about the last questions that had been troubling her. He had been planning this whole time. It was all starting to make sense to her as more and more of their trip had been revealed to her.

Thomas took the dress from her, putting it on a hanger that he held in his hand. "Wayan is going to steam this for you and she's also got someone waiting for you downstairs to do your nails and hair. Oh, and I almost forgot." He walked over to his closet to bring out a shoebox, taking off the lid and handing it to Isabella with a grin. "I think you'll find these acceptable. Well, the woman who picked them out told me that any woman would die to have these in her closet."

Isabella flung her arms around Thomas's neck. "I can't believe you've done all this. It's really such a surprise. I love it all. I can't wait to put it on."

Thomas had a mischievous grin on his face.

Isabella laughed. "What's that look for?"

"Yeah, about my present?"

Isabella nodded and made a funny face at him. "Yes, the present that I've not gotten for you yet."

"Seeing you in that dress tonight is going to be beyond any gift you could give me. You're going to look stunning, Iz."

"I love you so much. You're entirely too good to me, Thomas."

Thomas leaned in to wipe away the single tear that had slid down her cheek, and the way he was looking at her caused her heart to beat rapidly. He kissed her deeply on the lips before he pulled away. "I love you too, Iz. You're the best thing that's ever happened to me." A few seconds passed, the look between them genuine and more real than anything Isabella had ever dared to dream of. "Now go. Get ready so I can see you in that dress."

Isabella grinned and gave him one last quick kiss on the cheek. "Going!"

"Ready?" Isabella called downstairs to Thomas.

"I'm so ready to see you in that dress. Get down here, woman."

Isabella took one last look in the full-length mirror, smoothing her hair back with her hand and smiling at her reflection. She was thankful that at the last minute of her packing, she'd included her red lipstick and a small make-up bag with a few items that she sometimes applied for special occasions.

She started her descent down the stairway, fully aware of Thomas standing at the bottom waiting for her.

"Oh, Iz. Wow!"

The way he was looking at her was causing her heart to beat faster, and she hoped that the smile on her face matched the way that his admiration was making her feel—adored. She felt completely adored by Thomas. All the discussions and things that they'd worked through during the past few days slipped away from her thoughts. She promised in that moment to let go of her past mistakes and only focus on a future that she had with the man she loved.

"So you like it?" she teased him when she'd reached the bottom of the staircase, enjoying the almost stunned expression on his face.

"Uh, that would be the understatement of the year, I'd say." He took her hands in his as he stepped back a little, his eyes traveling down the length of her body to her carefully manicured toes and back up to her eyes and the smile that she knew stretched wide across her face. "Isabella, you look absolutely gorgeous."

She took a step toward him, kissing him lightly on the lips and then carefully wiping off the lipstick that she'd left behind at the corner of his mouth. "Why, thank you. And I love the dress. You did very well—or whomever you had helping you did very well." She laughed.

"Hey, I was pretty involved, I'll have you know."

"Were you?"

"Yes, I looked through many different photos of dresses that were sent to me before they'd gotten the color just right—and the neckline." He winked at her and Isabella laughed, her fingers automatically going to her cleavage.

"Can you guess my inspiration?"

"Yes, I think so." Isabella didn't know why, but she felt a little shy all of a sudden. "Maybe the dress I wore in London last year—the night you kissed me? The 'mistake kiss'." Isabella did air quotes around the words, and Thomas laughed as he grabbed her around the waist and pulled her to him.

"That kiss was just my wild fantasies coming to fruition, and it was you in that red dress you were wearing that made it impossible to hold back."

"Oh, is that so?" she said, enjoying their flirtation.

"And on that note, we better get going before I start to get other ideas. We have about a thirty-minute drive ahead of us, so plenty of time to admire you in the car." He placed her hand firmly at his elbow as he led her out to the car waiting for them outside.

THIRTY-TWO

Isabella looked across the table at Thomas as he lifted his glass of wine out in front of him. "To you, my lovely Isabella. Merry Christmas and thank you for giving me the best year of my life."

Isabella couldn't quite put her finger on it, but ever since they'd arrived at the restaurant, Thomas had suddenly gone slightly quiet. She was trying to push the thought out of her mind because everything was so beautiful—so perfect. She turned her attention to him as she clinked her glass with his.

"To us. And thank you for this wonderful dinner."

Thomas had really outdone himself, renting out an entire restaurant with an incredible view of the water. They could hear the waves crashing against the rocks below, and the moonlight filled up the sky perfectly. In one corner of the restaurant a string quartet played soft romantic music, and every bite of the seafood dishes they'd ordered had been spectacular.

Thomas held out his fork with a piece of chocolate cake on the end of it. "You've gotta try this."

"Okay, but it's the last bite of food that is going in my mouth tonight." She allowed him to feed her. "That was worth it. Wow. Everything was so delicious. We're going to have to run an extra mile in the morning." She laughed at the look on Thomas's face. "What? You already know that you're not going to run with me tomorrow?"

Thomas laughed. "We'll see. Or maybe we'll be sleeping in tomorrow." He winked and then seemed to be studying her for a good long while again.

She didn't miss the fact that he'd been running his fingers through his hair an awful lot during dinner. She laughed lightly and reached her hand across the table to his. "Thomas, what's up with you?"

"What?" He grinned at her.

"You know what? You know I can always tell when you've got something on your mind."

"You know me so well, huh?" He was grinning and then he got up from his chair to walk across the room to tell the waiter something.

Isabella watched him, curious about what was going on. He certainly had been full of surprises during their entire trip so far.

Thomas came back over to the table and leaned down to give her a kiss. He reached for her hand. "Come with me. Let's go for a little walk by the water."

Isabella took his hand and stood up. "Hmm. I'm not so sure about walking in these shoes." She didn't wear heels enough to be great in them to begin with, but she knew they wouldn't work for walking in the sand.

Thomas grinned. "It's okay. I have you covered." He gestured toward the top of the stairs that led down to the water and Isabella could see her favorite pair of flip-flops sitting there.

She laughed. "You really thought of everything."

She felt Thomas's hand tighten around hers as they neared the bottom of the stone steps. As they started walking to the right, Isabella could see a table set up under a beautiful canopy, and as they got closer she could see the champagne in the ice bucket and hear the violinist who had begun playing quietly off to the side.

"Thomas!" She looked up at him. "What is all this? You've really outdone yourself in the romance department tonight."

"You think? I hope so. I never want you to question how special you are to me."

"Thomas." She stopped and looked at him. "I'm absolutely the luckiest girl in the world right now. I can't believe that you've done all this."

They started walking again and when Isabella moved toward the chair, Thomas pulled her gently away to stand in the sand not far from the table, his eyes never leaving her face.

Isabella felt the tears behind her eyes. Before he even spoke a word, she could see the intensity on his face, the love that he had for her. A light breeze whipped her hair and he reached out to place it back behind her ears like he'd done a hundred times before, his light touch against her face making her shiver for wanting a kiss from him.

She leaned in to kiss him and then he took both of her hands in his, creating a little more space between them.

"A year ago today, I took a leap of faith when I went to you in Tuscany—to tell you things that I couldn't keep to myself any longer."

"To tell me that you loved me." Isabella could only whisper the words. It was an important day—she'd thought of it as their anniversary. It was the day that things had forever changed between her and her best friend. The day that she finally knew for certain that she wasn't alone in how she felt for Thomas. And now here he was, being so sweet to her, showing and telling her all day long that the day had held just as much meaning for him as it did for her.

"Yes. I remember telling you that night, after we kissed, that I had some things to say to you."

Isabella nodded. She could remember that night—the kiss and his words—just like it was yesterday.

He squeezed her hands a little tighter. "Well, Miss Isabella

Dawson, tonight I have some more things that I want to say to you."

His smile was so tender, and Isabella thought she could see a hint of tears glistening in his eyes as he took a deep breath.

"From the moment I met you all those years ago in science class, I never wanted to be apart from you. You were always the one person I could count on, without fail, to laugh at my jokes, and your friendship over the years has meant more to me than I could ever express.

"Finally realizing just a year ago that you are the only one for me—that I could never imagine my life without you in it—has altered my life in ways I could never have imagined."

Isabella's hands went to her mouth as Thomas got down on one knee in the sand in front of her. She could feel the tears starting and she was shaking a little as she watched him take a small box out of his pocket. As she looked at his face—so serious—the whole scene felt surreal to her for a few seconds, as if she actually needed to pinch herself to be sure that she wasn't dreaming.

Thomas opened the lid of the box and held it out in front of him so that Isabella could look down and see the most spectacular diamond ring she'd ever laid eyes on—not just because of the cut and size, but because of the person holding the ring out to her.

"Isabella Dawson, will you marry me?"

Isabella felt so stunned that she couldn't speak for a few seconds as she stared at Thomas holding the ring. "Yes! Yes, I'll marry you. Oh, Thomas!" Isabella flung herself into his arms, sobbing tears of joy as he held her and kissed her deeply before wiping all her tears away with his hand.

"You will? You'll be my wife?"

He was teasing her; she stuck her hand out in front of her so that he could place the ring on her finger.

"Thomas, it's gorgeous!" She held out her hand so that they could both admire the ring on her finger.

"You know what I think, Isabella Dawson?" Thomas took her face in both his hands as he leaned in to give her the sweetest kiss.

"What's that?" She whispered the question, hardly able to think, for all the overwhelming thoughts she was having.

"I think that you are the most gorgeous diamond-wearing kinda girl I've ever seen in my life. You, my love, make that ring look spectacular."

Isabella laughed, the memory of their not-so-long-ago shopping trip in San Francisco flashing through her mind.

"Thank you, Thomas—for making me the happiest girl in the world." She took his hand and placed it over her heart. "Can you feel how fast my heart is still beating? Oh..." The thought flickered through her mind. It was the perfect moment in Bali, but she hadn't been thinking of it when they'd left the villa earlier.

"What, Iz?"

"Oh, nothing. I was just thinking of Arianna's ashes. You know how I told you that I've been trying to spread them in locations that are important to me? Well..." She laughed lightly. "I'm pretty sure that this spot is going to take a prize in that regard— but it's okay."

Her eyes widened as she realized what Thomas had taken out of his pocket.

"You brought them." She felt the sting of tears for the sweetness in that he'd thought to do so.

"Well, I figured that, assuming you and I were in agreement about you becoming my wife and all, this might be one of those special moments that you'd want to share with her." He handed her the small box and kissed her on the cheek. "You go. I'll pour our champagne."

Isabella took the box and kissed him on the cheek. "I won't be long. And thank you, Thomas."

THIRTY-THREE

Isabella took a sip of her champagne. What a magical night it had been! She never would have dreamed that she'd be sitting there as an engaged woman at the end of the night. Everything had happened so fast that she hadn't had a chance to wrangle all the questions that were now swimming around in her head.

Thomas grinned at her. "I know that look. What are you thinking about?"

"Oh, I'm just thinking that I can't believe you're no longer my boyfriend." She held out her hand so that she could admire the ring. "I, Isabella Dawson, now have a fiancé. Oh, Thomas. We have to call our parents. I can't wait to tell them. Won't they all be so pleased?"

Thomas made a funny face.

Isabella laughed. "So, I'm guessing they already know."

"Well, that would have been one of those phone calls you were getting so angry at me about." Thomas winked. "In all seriousness, of course I wanted to ask your father for your hand in marriage—which I admit took some bribery."

Isabella laughed. "Oh, stop. My parents love you."

"Well, we both know that hasn't always been the case. But yes, your parents seemed quite pleased." Thomas lifted an eyebrow. "Iz, what's going on in that head of yours? Not having second thoughts, are you?"

Isabella reached across the table to grab his hand. "Don't be silly. I was just thinking about next week—your leaving. There's no way that I'm not going back with you, Thomas. I'll just have to make it work in New York. I mean, it's different now, right? We can travel together later and we can plan a great honeymoon."

"Iz?"

"Yeah?"

"I might have one more surprise for you."

"Okay." Isabella couldn't imagine what else he could possibly say to surprise her.

"What would you say if I told you that I'm not going back to New York?" Thomas was grinning at her.

"What do you mean?"

"I mean that I want to stay with you—in Thailand, in Bali—or wherever else we might decide to go."

"What about school? What are you not telling me? I knew something was up with you about school."

Thomas laughed. "I decided to try doing an online semester. I'm not leaving NYU. I'll just be doing my coursework virtually. So, I will be somewhat busy, but as long as we have wi-fi, I figure I can make it work. Well, that is, if you don't think it would be cramping your style."

"Are you kidding me? This is my dream come true right now. I mean, pinch me, because I must seriously be dreaming."

Thomas took a last sip of champagne and stood up to come around to Isabella's side, reaching for her hand as he helped her out of her chair. He wrapped his arms around her waist and looked into her eyes. "I love you, Iz. I want our every day to be a great adventure together."

"I love you too. You make me so happy, Thomas. You have no idea."

. . .

During the ride back to the villa, curled up on the backseat of the car together, they discussed their future. The whole night felt completely surreal to Isabella. It was everything she'd ever dared to dream of with Thomas.

Once they'd stopped to take a break from talking and kissing, they called first Isabella's parents and then Thomas's to share the news and wish them a Merry Christmas. Isabella also called her birth father, Lucas, in San Francisco and had a hard time getting off the phone with five-year old Annie once the topic of being a flower girl had been mentioned.

Isabella nuzzled closer to Thomas's chest. "Oh, I can't wait to phone everyone in Tuscany. They're going to be so happy, right? Or do they know too?" Isabella laughed.

"No. No one else knows. I thought I'd save that for you to share." Thomas looked at the time on his phone. "Let's see, maybe we should give them a few hours. They're probably having their Christmas dinner right about now." He tilted her chin up so that he could give her a kiss. "Do you think we can occupy ourselves for a few hours?"

Isabella nodded, content to lie against Thomas's chest for the remainder of the ride back to the villa—beautiful images of travel, weddings, and future children filling her head.

THIRTY-FOUR

Isabella rubbed her eyes as she sat up. "I guess I was tired."

"Babe, you were out ten minutes into the movie."

They'd decided to put a movie on when they'd gotten back to the villa, wanting to wait for a good time to call everyone in Italy. Now, nestled close together with Thomas on the sofa, the impact of everything hit Isabella once again. They were going to be married.

"What's causing that smile on your pretty little face?"

Thomas was rubbing her back in a circular motion, causing her to second-guess the idea she'd had to get up from the sofa. "Mmm. That feels so good."

He kissed her. "Does it?"

She grinned at him and nodded. "Is this what I have to look forward to every day of my life?"

"Possibly. If you remain so cute and good to me."

They both laughed, and Isabella finally stood up.

"Shall we call them now? I think it's probably as good a time as any to try," Thomas said.

"Can you give me ten minutes?"

"Sure. I've got some e-mails to respond to."

Isabella walked upstairs to the bedroom, stopping on the way in to grab her backpack. She climbed up on the bed and pulled the journal out of the bag. It was Arianna's—the blue leather one—the first words she'd ever read from her birth mother.

She turned to the letter that she'd been thinking about all night, the vision of Thomas's face as he'd looked at her in the moonlight forever etched into her memory.

I want for you to know love, Bella—to give your heart to another for all eternity.

If I have any regrets, my biggest one is that I didn't live long enough to know the true love of my soulmate. I didn't know what it was like to have an open heart until the end of my days. I'd spent too much of my short life guarded, being afraid to let someone in who could make me feel the pain of potential loss.

Take chances with your heart when you know deep in your soul that the one looking into your eyes loves you like no other.

Be brave and courageous when it comes to love, Bella. Experience it deeply without holding back.

Isabella felt the full impact of the words her mother had written to her. Her heart *was* completely open to Thomas and she had no doubts about Thomas's love for her, about the way that he looked at her. She thought about how happy Arianna would have been for her and how much she would have loved Thomas.

Isabella's heart was full, and she was the happiest that she'd ever been in her entire life.

She smiled as she looked at the one picture of Arianna that she'd tucked inside the journal. It *was* sad that her birth mother hadn't lived long enough to know true love, but Isabella wouldn't dwell on that. She'd focus on what Arianna had wanted for her and be content to know how happy she would have been for Isabella.

She closed the journal and wiped away one single tear before she headed back downstairs to where Thomas was waiting for her.

THIRTY-FIVE

Isabella squeezed Thomas's hand tight as they waited for the video chat to connect. She could hardly contain the excitement that she felt about telling everyone their news. Thomas leaned over and kissed her just as Lia's face appeared on the laptop screen.

"Well, hello, you lovebirds." Her grandmother, Lia, was laughing and soon joined by Isabella's grandfather beside her.

"Merry Christmas, you two. We sure do miss you here," Antonio said.

"Merry Christmas. We miss you too." Isabella grinned into the screen. "Have you had a nice dinner?"

"We have, yes. I'm sure we'll be passing you around to everyone soon, but let me lift the laptop up so everyone can see your beautiful face," Antonio said.

Isabella heard Lia in the background. "Shh, everyone. It's Bella and Thomas."

Isabella felt tears as she saw them all seated around the table, grinning and shouting out "Merry Christmas" to them—Gigi and Douglas, Blu and Chase, Jemma and Rafael, and a smaller table with all the kids. They were all there, celebrating with one another and happy to have Isabella as part of their special family.

The screen settled in on Gigi and Douglas at the table.

"Merry Christmas, Bella. We miss you and love you so much, honey. Merry Christmas, Thomas," Gigi was saying into the screen.

"I love you too. Gigi, can you please have Antonio hold up the screen again?" She and Thomas looked at one another before she looked back into the camera, sure that the huge grin on her face was going to give away her surprise. "Thomas and I have a little announcement we'd like to share with you all."

Moments later, she could again make out everyone sitting at the table.

"Merry Christmas, everyone. I wanted to share with you all the beautiful gift I got from this amazing guy over here." She laughed, putting the camera fully on Thomas, who waved at everyone.

She grinned into the camera, held out her hand, turning it so that the ring practically filled up the screen. "We're getting married! Thomas asked me to be his wife!" She couldn't keep the tears from flowing as she saw the reactions around the room for a split second before Lia's face filled the screen again—with Jemma, Gigi, and Blu quickly crowding in behind her on the screen.

They were all wiping away tears, and Lia seemed to be having a hard time getting her words together.

"Oh honey, that's the best news ever. Congratulations, you two," Antonio said.

"Bella! I'm so happy for you, girl. We need to talk—and plan," Jemma chimed in, with the biggest grin on her face.

"And it goes without saying that I'll happily be designing your dress," Blu said.

Finally Lia seemed to be ready to speak, and by this time Isabella could barely talk herself for all of the emotions she was feeling after seeing everyone so happy for her.

"Bella, we can do the wedding here—at the villa. Please tell me you will. It will be so gorgeous—you will be so gorgeous—and it can be whatever you want—"

"—And Lia and I will help you with everything." Gigi's face was suddenly there beside Lia's as she wiped tears away from her eyes. "Oh, this is just the best news ever."

Isabella was laughing now, finally able to talk herself. She looked at Thomas. "Lia, we were hoping that you'd say that we could have it there. I can't think of a better place for our wedding. And I'm sure it will be absolutely perfect, but mostly because of having you all there with us for the occasion."

Finally, after everyone had said their congratulations and things had calmed down a bit, Antonio appeared back in front of the screen, handing a glass of champagne to Lia. "Thomas, my good man..." He winked into the camera. "Please tell me that you have something worthy of a toast on hand for your lovely bride-to-be."

Thomas laughed. "In fact I do." He motioned to Wayan, who appeared seemingly out of nowhere with two glasses of champagne.

Thomas handed one to Isabella and took the other in his own hand as they waited for Antonio to speak.

Antonio held out his glass and Isabella could see everyone behind him doing the same.

"To Bella and Thomas...may the love you feel for one another now, grow only stronger every day."

Shouts of "cheers" could be heard from around the room.

Isabella finished her goodbyes and closed the laptop. She felt Thomas pull her back down on the sofa next to him. She turned her face slightly so that she could see his face. "Thomas?"

"Yeah?"

"You do realize that you've kinda set yourself up here in terms of Christmas surprises."

Thomas laughed. "You have a good point. Maybe I should go on the record now as saying that I'm not so sure that I have many more surprises left in me."

"Oh, I kinda doubt that." Isabella lifted her head so that she could kiss him on the lips. "I have the feeling that our lives together are going to be filled with surprises."

Thomas smiled back at her. "I think you just might be right about that."

She felt Thomas's sweet kiss on her head and heard the words that he whispered as her cheek nestled back against his chest and her eyes closed.

"I'll love you forever, Iz."

———

THE STORY CONTINUES

Bella's Home
Legacy Series, Book 10

Available on Amazon

PaulaKayBooks.com

BELLA'S HOME — PREVIEW

Chapter 1

Isabella turned slightly so that she could see herself in the full-length mirror, gasping a little when she saw her reflection.

"Is that a good sign or a bad one?" Blu said, taking a pin from between her lips to place it where she was cinching the satin material at Isabella's waist.

Before Isabella could reply, she heard Gigi's own gasp from the doorway, followed by Lia's right after.

"Bella, you're so beautiful!" Gigi said.

"We've been counting down the days to see you in this dress." Lia walked over to where Isabella stood on a small stool to take her hand, and Isabella didn't miss the tears in her eyes.

Isabella laughed lightly. "I know. We've kept you all waiting a good long time, haven't we?"

Lia squeezed her hand. "Oh, I don't know. There's nothing wrong with a long engagement."

"Speak for yourself." Gigi winked. "I was beginning to wonder if Douglas and I would—you know—still be around for the wedding day."

"Gi, you're so silly. You and Douglas aren't going anywhere. Well, Douglas isn't anyway—not the way he ran that five miles with me yesterday." Isabella laughed and Gigi leaned in to kiss her on the cheek.

"You have a point there. That man is in the best shape I've seen him in since we were married—despite all the wonderful food Lia's always cooking for us," said Gigi.

"It's the Tuscan air." Lia smiled at Gigi. "And our morning walks are paying off for you too. Don't pretend that you're not feeling—and looking—pretty wonderful yourself, young lady."

Isabella looked back down at Blu and the two smiled at one another—it was the silent shared acknowledgment of how great it always felt to be all together.

"Well? I'm still waiting on your thoughts there, little miss bride-to-be. There's still a lot of work to be done, of course, but what do you think so far?"

"Ooh, it's better than I ever imagined. Thank you again—so much, Blu—for making my dress—for making all the dresses for me. I still can't believe that you really have the time."

Blu winked at her. "I'll always make time for you and—well, to repeat Gigi's point, I've had a few years to play with the sketches."

They all laughed and Isabella pulled her hair back away from her face as she looked into the mirror at herself and the other women sitting nearby. "Well, you know me. We wanted to wait until Thomas was finished with school—until we had a good idea of where we'd end up once we were married."

Isabella didn't miss the look that passed between Lia and Gigi. "Wait. What's that look for, you two?"

"Oh, nothing," said Gigi.

Blu took the final pin out from between her lips and whispered loud enough for everyone in the room to hear. "Every time you leave the villa, these two talk about how much they want you to stay forever."

"Believe me, it's hard for me to leave too," said Isabella.

Over the past few years, since she and Thomas had gotten engaged, they'd spent Christmases and most of the summers at Lia's and Antonio's. After some fantastic European vacations, Isabella's parents had surprised everyone when they'd decided to sell their house in Connecticut to move to a sweet little village on the coast of Spain. And they too, would often come to Tuscany to stay in one of the many guest houses that Lia and Antonio had added to their property.

When Isabella stopped to think about it, it was a little odd that she and Thomas would be choosing to settle down in Connecticut after all their travels, but she felt that she had to support his decisions when it came to his career.

Thomas had always supported her throughout the years, and Isabella had done her share of waffling back and forth when it came to her settling in New York City. Finally, she'd gotten an apartment and spent time in the city near Thomas about as much as she did away traveling. And they'd made it work, Thomas getting through his studies and Isabella marking off the spots on Arianna's map.

She grinned thinking about the map. She'd brought it with her to Italy. Gigi, especially, always seemed to enjoy looking at it with her—hearing about her adventures as Isabella shared pictures and stories about her travels.

"Sorry, what did you say, Gigi?"

Gigi laughed, probably at the funny expression on Isabella's face as she'd zoned out thinking about everything under the sun.

"I was just reminding you that I want to see the pictures of the house."

Isabella nodded. "Oh, yes. I have them on my phone."

"How many bedrooms did you say it has?"

"Four bedrooms and an apartment above the garage." This time Isabella definitely saw a look pass between Gigi and Lia. She laughed. "Yes, I know. Plenty of room for an expanding family."

"Well, it can't hurt to be ready." Lia grinned at Isabella.

Isabella's thoughts turned back to Thomas and their new home. He'd gone to so much trouble to find just the right house for them—a house that Isabella would love. And she had loved it when she'd seen it—she'd agreed that living there, a doable commute from what would be Thomas's new office, made sense for them.

Thomas would be working in management for his father's company and Isabella could write from anywhere—Thomas had said that they'd set up the space above the garage to be her office. And they'd keep Isabella's apartment in the city—for Thomas's business meetings there and also as a place they could go to when they wanted a little getaway from the slower pace of the suburbs.

Without meaning to, Isabella sighed loud enough that all the women in the room turned to look at her.

"You okay? You're probably about ready to get out of that, huh?" Blu asked her.

Isabella turned to look out the nearby window. "Well, I think the guys will be in soon. Thomas and I have a date to go over the final items we need to do here before we leave for New York."

"Where'd they go so early this morning?" asked Gigi.

"I think Antonio wanted to go look at that property just up for sale." Lia winked at Gigi. "You know, the one I was saying that you and Douglas should think about."

Gigi laughed. "You mean, the vineyard next door to you? I don't want to speak for that energetic husband of mine, but I'm pretty confident that learning the fine art of wine-making is not a challenge we're up for at this stage in our lives."

Isabella grinned at them. "Lia, I don't think you'll be happy until we are all moved in right here with you at the vineyard."

Lia laughed too. "Well, I'd say you got that right. But okay, I'll settle for having Gigi in town. Now, my Bella so far away in Connecticut—that's another story, my dear."

Isabella felt a little wave of sadness. It was how she always felt when she it was time to leave Tuscany. "I know. But I'll be back before you know it. There's still too much to do to stay away for long."

Lia crossed the room to give Isabella a light kiss on the cheek. "You pay no attention to me, my dear. I know your priorities are right. Thomas is lucky to have you there supporting him and his career. We'll just have to take your visits when we can get them."

Blu had stepped back with a critical look on her face as she examined Isabella in the dress. "Well, it sure sounds like the newly-weds will have room for us in the new house. Not to invite ourselves, but I wouldn't say no to a visit." She winked at Isabella.

"Oh, you know I will love to have you all come visit. I'm going to hold you to that." Isabella turned to Lia as she took Blu's hand to step down from where Blu had been working on her dress. "And Lia, you will always be a priority for me—for both of us. We love coming here, and that's not going to stop after we're married."

Lia reached out to squeeze Isabella's hand. "I know, honey. Your grandfather and I are delighted with how often you visit. You just focus on that lovely husband-to-be. Speaking of which, Antonio just texted me that they are on their way home, so let's get you out of that dress."

Isabella followed Blu behind the partition she'd set up, hugging her tight before she stepped out of the dress. "The dress is really gorgeous. I can't express to you how much I love it. I feel just like a princess."

"As you should, lovely girl." Blu looked her in the eyes. "I can't wait to see the look on your young man's face when he sees you. You're going to be a beautiful bride, Bella."

Isabella smiled as Blu left her to change back into her clothes. She still had to pinch herself about the fact that she was marrying Thomas—the man of her dreams and the best friend she'd ever had.

Chapter 2

Gigi set the coffee down in front of her friend at the small breakfast table that overlooked the vineyard outside. Since moving to Tuscany two years ago, she and Lia had gotten into the wonderful routine of having coffee together at least a few mornings every week. The two women had only grown closer over the years, and Gigi could hardly imagine a time when they'd not known one another.

She reached across the table to place her hand on Lia's as her friend looked out the window, seemingly lost in her own thoughts. "Lia, are you okay? I can hold down the fort here if you want to go have a rest."

Lia smiled back at her. "Thank you. We'll just take a break here with our coffee for a few minutes and I'll be just fine. So, how stunning did our Bella look in that dress?"

Gigi felt her eyes instantly go wet with tears. Seeing Isabella in her wedding gown had literally taken her breath away. "I still don't know how Blu manages to do that, but it's the most gorgeous dress I've ever seen. And—well, Bella would look beautiful, no matter the dress, but indeed she looks like something out of the pages of a young girl's fairy tale."

"That's exactly what I was thinking." Lia nodded her head toward where the men stood talking outside in the vineyard not far from the house. "That young man is in for a wonderful treat."

Gigi nodded, also watching Thomas from the window as he grinned at the two men who'd seemed to become pretty important in his life since his engagement to Isabella.

"Douglas thinks the world of Thomas. The way that he jumped right in to help him with the rebuilding last summer said an awful lot about his character."

While Isabella and Thomas had been spending the previous summer at the vineyard, a terrible storm had done a lot of destruction to several of the main buildings at the orphanage. When Douglas had made plans to immediately fly to Guatemala, Thomas had been right beside him, no questions asked.

Lia was nodding in agreement. "Yes, Antonio also feels nothing but happy for Thomas to be joining our family officially." Lia looked across the table at Gigi, and Gigi didn't miss the gleam in her eye as she spoke her next words. "Antonio says that Thomas has a real knack for the business. He's very quick to pick things up and his interest has only seemed to grow stronger over the past year."

"I hope he'll be happy working for his father," said Gigi. "That it's what he really wants to do, I mean."

"Yes, that's exactly what Antonio and I have talked about. It's not our place to pry, and Bella doesn't share too much about it. She seems happy, though—with their plans—do you think so, Gigi?"

Gigi was thoughtful. They'd all been pretty careful when it came to Isabella's and Thomas's relationship. Isabella had shared with them some angst that she'd felt over the past years whenever she'd been living in New York City. It didn't feel like home to her, and the struggle had always been about how much time to spend there with Thomas versus traveling or spending time abroad with her family. In the end, of course, it was their decision to make, and Isabella's family understood her feelings of wanting to support Thomas with his career goals.

Gigi looked back over at Lia, who was waiting for a response from her. "Yes, I think she's happy with their plans." Gigi trusted that, more than anything, Thomas wanted Isabella to be happy. They'd work it out and the family would continue to enjoy long holidays and vacations together when they could.

Blu walked across the room, carrying her own cup of coffee to the table. "Ah, great minds think alike." She bent down to give Lia a quick hug and then leaned in to kiss Gigi on the cheek before joining the women at the table. She grinned over at them both. "Is it just me, or was Bella absolutely breathtaking in that dress? I mean, not to toot my own horn or anything." She smiled as she glanced down at the pictures she'd taken on her phone. "I have to say it..." She held her phone out, first for Gigi to see and then Lia. "Does she not look just like Ari?"

Lia smiled back at Blu. "I was thinking exactly the same thing about my beautiful granddaughter."

"The fact that we get to celebrate such a wonderful occasion with her feels a little bit like a miracle, doesn't it?" Gigi said.

So many years had passed since Arianna's death. Mostly now when they talked about her, Gigi was able to do so with fond memories and less sadness. Having Isabella in their lives years later had helped to heal so much of the remnants of the grief they'd all carried.

Lia smiled and looked out the window toward Antonio. "Yes, she's most definitely a miracle to us. One that I will be forever grateful for."

Blu, never one to hide her emotions, was watching Lia. Gigi could read the concern in her eyes as Blu reached her hand out to touch Lia gently on the arm.

"Lia, how are you doing? You'd tell us, wouldn't you? If it's too much having us all here?"

Lia was just as quick to show Blu a big smile. "Nonsense. I'm fine and everything is good. Having you all here is exactly what I need right now, so don't even for a second think that it's not the case."

"Okay, but we're here to help. Don't forget that. And Chase is arriving tomorrow with big plans for a dinner feast. I think you're really going to like the latest additions to his menu at the restaurant. He's been dying to make them for you."

Lia smiled. "I can't wait." She glanced toward the clock on the wall behind her. "Let's see...Emily and Richard are due here any minute. And Chase will be here with the girls by late afternoon. Is that right?"

"Yes, he told me today that Gabby and Kylie have had the best week at camp—so much so that they've been begging to go for another session," Blu said.

Lia laughed. "Yes, Gabriela mentioned that to me on the phone as well. I told her we'd talk about it after we've had her home for at least the weekend."

"Right. I was thinking, though, that it might make good sense for our trip down south. We could go for the first three weeks or so and then Chase or Antonio could bring the girls down for the rest of the time."

"So does this mean that you got the house you were telling us about? The one with the incredible view?" Gigi said.

"The one with the incredible kitchen?" Lia winked.

"I did indeed," said Blu. "It's going to be spectacular, with plenty of room for all of us and more to spare. It will be the perfect place for me to work on finishing the dresses, and I've already talked to Jemma. She's coming a few days after we arrive and I think she really wants it to be a surprise for Isabella."

"Well, I guess that's the question of the day, really." Gigi took a sip of her coffee. "Have you said anything to Bella yet?"

"Aha. I knew my ears were burning for a reason." Isabella laughed as she walked across the room to take the last available seat at the table. She turned toward Gigi. "Has who said what to me?"

Blu grinned and leaned over to give Isabella a quick hug. "Well, I—we, really—wanted to surprise you with a little getaway. I know that you've not really spent that much time at the Amalfi Coast, and I've rented the most beautiful big villa for us all in Positano for several weeks. We figured that it could be an extended wedding shower of sorts for you. We'll eat lovely food and drink lovely wine and I'll finish the dresses—"

"—Which will also be quite lovely." Lia laughed as she interrupted her friend.

"And Bella, I know you're planning to head back after the weekend, but we're hoping that you can change your plans—maybe just stay here with us until the wedding," Blu grinned.

Gigi was watching Isabella carefully. She saw the way the young girl's face lit up when Blu mentioned the Amalfi Coast, but she also knew that Isabella and Thomas had some major things to take care of back home, not the least of which was the closing on their new home in Connecticut. And she knew the look of Isabella's trying to hold back tears. That was the look that she saw now.

"You all are so sweet to do this. Any other time, I'd jump at the chance, but I just don't see how I could make that happen. We've got to get back to pack up the remaining things from my apartment and close on the house. Maybe I can come out a few weeks earlier if you're still there? But I shouldn't say yes until I speak to Thomas about it. I know that he had some other things that he wanted us to get done before we come back out for the wedding, and—well, I have been traveling already a lot this year." She laughed lightly. "I don't want him to feel that I'm choosing travel —or Italy—over him every time."

Blu leaned over to give Isabella a hug. "Don't worry, Bella. We knew that it might not work with your plans, and I understand. Talk to Thomas and just let us know if anything will work for you. Gigi, Lia, and I will be there for the month, and it's looking like the kids will come join us for the last week or so—after their camp lets out."

Gigi reached across the table to squeeze Isabella's hand. "Talk to Thomas, and only if it feels like the right thing to do, okay, honey?"

Isabella nodded her head and stood up to walk over to the window, her face lighting up in a big smile. "My parents are here!"

A NOTE FROM THE AUTHOR

Thank you so much for reading *Bella's Heart*.

If you've fallen in love with these characters and the world of the Legacy Series, I'd love to invite you deeper into the story.

I've written a quiet, emotional prequel titled *Out of Time* that sheds light on the relationships, choices, and moments that shaped everything that follows.

As a thank-you for joining my reader list, you can receive *Out of Time* as a free digital gift, along with future updates and special releases from the Legacy Series and my other women's fiction.

To receive your free prequel, please visit:
PaulaKayBooks.com

I'm so glad you're here.
—Paula

ABOUT THE AUTHOR

Paula Kay writes women's fiction about family, friendship, and the quiet moments that shape who we become.

Her Legacy Series explores love, loss, and the ties that bind us across generations, with settings inspired by Italy, San Francisco, and the places that feel like home long after we've left them behind.

When she's not writing, Paula enjoys meaningful conversations, books that make her cry, and a little too much reality television.

PaulaKayBooks.com

ALSO BY PAULA KAY

Rock the Boat

Back on Track